CW01521887

Outside of a Dog

InkyLab Anthology No.2

'Outside of a dog, a book is man's best friend; inside of a dog it's too dark to read.'

Groucho Marx

First published in 2020 by InkyLab Ltd.
ISBN 978-1-9162594-1-6
Printed by Book Printing UK
Front cover design by P. Miller
Back cover illustration by Johnny O
Edited by G. Bartaby and D. Totton

Contents

Foreword

Hurrah!

Well, we made it to our second anthology! And we have a whole seething potful of new stories for you to enjoy!

But first - we'll let that simmer for a while - thanks must go out to everyone who's helped us get this thing on the boil. To all our writers, who have been wonderfully supportive, and in particular to Jane Carnaffan, who has been scouring the land like a one-woman plague of librivorous locusts to help us sell and promote the anthology - we'd be nowhere without you, Jane! - and to Sara Waymont, who secured us our recent radio interview on British Forces Broadcasting Service, in anticipation of our forthcoming Remembrance Day edition (a long way off, I know, but we'll get there!). Many thanks to both of you.

Also to Dylan Totton, for his assistance in co-editing and promoting this current anthology, and his level-headedness in the face of our rather more pig-headed disputations.

But back to the pot. We've been cooking up a stew of stories on the theme of books and literature, and it's a hearty dish. We've lovely bits of crime fiction from Jane and quasi-fantasy from Sara, mixed in with light-hearted muted dithyrambics from Aurora Cording and K Weismann - who seem to be in some kind of competition as to who can write the most rambling, futile dialogue (they definitely are, I overheard them in the Black Garter!) - and of course a pinch of weird spice from Johnny O. Along with our other regulars and a couple of new ingredients it makes for a pretty satisfactory repast, we'd say. But enough of my culinary witterings, grab a spoon and judge for yourself!*

Bon appetit!

InkyLab

*Please don't try to eat this book with a spoon...

Calm Down Café and the Voodoo Writer
(Arse Longa, Wiener Brevis)

K Weismann

'I am a weaver of dreams!' he proclaimed.

And a talker of shite!

In the effervescent crucible of miscreation that was his mind he was a Caesar or Alexander. An empire-building, world-straddling colossus (though he couldn't even quote Shakespeare correctly), tracing his lineage back through a whole slew of heroes, statesmen, poets, and thinkers to some divine coupling between Zeus and a cafetière. In the ungodly flesh he was a lesser Private Walker. A triple-jointed, fly-by-night pretender to the throne in his teapot demi-monde.

Of course, I was not to know that at the time. But I was about to find out.

*

'Twenty quid to anyone who completes the training by the end of the week!'

I did.

And he did. Twenty quid. *Da-da-dum.*

*

'Nice handwriting! Can you draw? Can you make me a sign?'

I did.

And he did. Twenty quid. *Da-da-dum.*

*

'Read a book when it's quiet.'

Da-da-dum.

'Doodle pictures on walls.'

Da-da-dum.

'Have a pizza, it's yours.'

Da-da-dum.

'Wear your Withnail T-shirt, it lends character - we're relaxed and we're anything goes.'

*

And so he painted himself as some Panglossian paragon of the World Perfect. What he said, he did. His promises were as good as signed in gold.

I worked in Calm Down Café, the coolest teahouse in the world, with the best boss ever.

*

So when he said I don't have your wages right now, I'll give you them on your next shift, I said cool, see you soon.

I never had another shift. I never saw the man again.

Davy Smallwill - let's have some backdrop on the bugger, from the point of view of retrospection, since I'm clearly never going to see him again. Davy Smallwill. He had a finger in every pie. Which is to say like all other malodorous pie-fingerers he thought he knew What Was Going On. He had his finger On The Pulse. Of course, having your finger on the pulse and having a finger in every pie do not equate to the same thing, even if one of the pies is a Really Nice Pie. Really Nice Pie it may be, but - natural laws prevailing - it's unlikely to have a pulse. And whether or no, you've ruined it by sticking your greedy fat finger in it. No one wants your fingered pie, Davy!

Davy, Davy. What an arse. Davy Smallwill. Smallwilly to his friends. Friends? OK, acquaintances. He must have friends, I suppose, although who these people are I cannot imagine. People who have never had to trust him with anything. People who've never lent him a tenner. Who've never asked a favour that wasn't mutually beneficial. People who haven't known him longer than three months.

Probably just people who are arseholes themselves. Cos let's not mince our words here, guys. Yes, I could dress it up in apophthegms and lace, but far more simple and to-the-point to say: 'The man's an arsehole. His friends are all arseholes.' We all know the kind of people we're dealing with.

People who'd give you the nickname Smallwilly.

People who'd relate what follows.

As said, I never saw him again. What follows on his account is what I was told by third parties.

But back to the point.

Davy Smallwilly. It galled him, the sobriquet. For obvious reasons. The most obvious and the most galling being it was true. A curled and crusty nub of a thing it was, like some kind of mollusc. A third-rate cuckold's horn - ironic, given that his girlfriend, as secretary to some trumped-up little MEP or other, was frequently 'away on business in Europe' - or the tip of a Turk's slipper put on too hot a wash. Supposedly it was at school in PE it was noticed, howled about the changing rooms and whooped throughout the whole school. *'S like a big clit! Y' gorra slug in yer fanny?* Maybe. Myself, I can't imagine the name didn't suggest itself of its own accord, regardless of the facts. His name is Smallwill, for fuck's sake! What puerile mind wouldn't extrapolate from that to Smallwilly?

Ho ho, you say. *Très drôle.* Anything else? Um... Runs a teahouse, thinks he's the Emperor Hadrian with his scraggly hipster beard, dick... No, not really, no. Nothing which hasn't been said.

Onward, then.

When I started at Calm Down Café it was run by a hippyish bloke named Rob, who also had a bakery round the corner, which made all the cakes and pastries and pizzas and what-have-you sold in the café. He was very relaxed, very laid-back. Unfortunately, so laid-back that the café fell flat on its arse. He sold it to Davy; swapped it for a clapped-out Morris Traveller or a bag of Frazzles or something. Davy promised big things. The world in an espresso cup. Needless to say, the world stalwartly refused to be shoehorned into an espresso cup. I don't know the specific details, don't really care either. I can imagine.

I can envisage his febrile little mind bubbling with whys and wherefores right now. The cup broke, had to be replaced, but could only be purchased - for authenticity - by the hundredweight from an artisan potter chucking his mud about somewhere in a bunion of a village on the toe of Italy and shipped - in a family tradition dating back two thousand years - by trireme past Scylla and Charybdis and through the Pillars of Hercules. Hercules, distracted, dropped the world and - would you believe it! - it landed on the café. The café had to be refurbished, in a stotties-'n'-pease-pudding motif, natch, and by traditional Tyneside dockers, of course, to the continuous rambling blether of 'The Blaydon Races'. For authenticity. The dockers, being on average a hundred and thirty two years of age, worked at a rate of one chair leg per calendar month collectively, and the renovation was due to be completed by the 33rd of Neverember, 2027. Also, the shoehorn had been bent in the process. And you can only imagine how difficult shoehorns are to come by!

That I can, Davy, that I can. You Janus-faced, finagling little reptile, you.

Howsoever, that makes no never-mind to me. You owe me four hundred quid.

But I've got bills to pay!

And employees too, no less.

I'll get it to you, I promise.

That you will, sunbeam. That you will.

A week rolled by, then another and another, accreting moulding layers of lost time, day after day the same, like the back-and-forth texts, day after day the same, like the beetle with his dung, like Sisyphus with his rock, and to as much avail.

I worked on those texts! Oh, I'd found another job, don't worry, I was OK on that account. But I put most of my energy into pithy texts. I may never get my money, but he'd damn well know what I thought of him. I worked it into poetry.

This oily man, so Janus-faced
I curse him - but with what?

With what, though? What, though? What, though? WHAT
Would rhyme with Janus-faced?

Or should it be:

I curse you, squamous one!
Ophidian and Janus-faced
A fitting curse, but what?
Now what would rhyme with Janus-faced?

Prose too. Between lattes and macchiatos I'd scribble notes on the backs of discarded kitchen orders. True, I had nothing concrete as yet, just a drawer full of scraps of paper, but when I did get around to assembling it - *oho!* - it would be the wittiest and most excoriating satire, yes it would, withering it would be, lambasting Davy and all his kind and exposing them for the grubby little fraudsters they really were. I'd publish it and the world would see him stripped bare. You may have beaten me today, Davy, but your comeuppance will be indelibly stamped in ink for all time. Ho ho ho!

It was 9:45pm when Davy finally quit the office. A long day. Stripping the staff right back to just his chef had meant coming in to help in the café in the morning before work, and taking an extended lunch break likewise. It had saved him on wages but cost him in additional nerve-wrangling. He couldn't have wound up more frazzled if he'd stuck his fingers directly into the mains supply. Plus he'd had to make up the shortfall by staying late to catch up on the papers he'd missed throughout the day. And still he had the cups and the fairtrade coffee beans to sort out. And the wallpapering, and the stockroom. Plus the dishwasher needed repairing. And Olly was demanding a proper hob.

    Flippety-balls! Olly. He'd almost forgotten. Well, Connie was away in the Hague at least for the fortnight so there was no rush home. Still, it meant another hour or two before he'd get home, and he could already feel a headache coming on. Nothing to be done about it, though, he'd said he'd drop by and talk things over. *Ohhh...* He turned left as he exited the building and left the Audi where it was. It should be fine, they never remembered to lock the barriers anyway. He cut through the back streets and up through the square, up past the café - he checked the locks just to be on the safe side - and into The Squeaking Wheel.

He ordered two-thirds of a pint of Jodhpur - an excellent IPA, hoppy and light with a crisp mouthfeel, but strong, and he was driving after all, and what with this incipient headache... He scanned the bar. It was busy for a Tuesday, but he finally found Olly by one of the speaker stacks.

'Hey, man!' He pulled up a spare stool.

'Finally!' - there was a lilt of three hours' drinking to the timbre of Olly's voice - 'Where the fuck've you been?'

'Sorry mate, had to stay late. I thought I'd said.'

'Yeah, I didn't think you meant *this* late. I thought you meant like eight or so.'

'That was the plan. There was more to do than I anticipated. And there's still more.' Davy sipped his Jodhpur and licked his lips - *Like some kind of gecko*, Olly thought. 'And I still haven't had chance to sort through any of the stuff for the café.'

'You need to sort that fucking kitchen.' It was both matter-of-fact and minatory. 'It needs fixing. Environmental Health will close us down *on the spot* if they drop in.'

'I know, I know,' Davy sighed. 'It could do with a refurb.'

'It could *do*,' Olly stated, 'with ripping out.'

'You know I don't have the money to do that.'

'Don't replace it and you won't even have a café.'

'It's not that bad.'

'There's some kind of slime growing in the dishwasher that looks like the kind of shit you see on deep-sea vents.'

'I'll look into it.'

'I wouldn't. You might come out without a face.'

'I'll sort it.'

'Y'know, I could do half this stuff myself if you left me another member of staff to cover.'

'I can't afford it.'

'It'd save you in the long run.'

'Trade at present doesn't warrant another member of staff. I can manage. I'll help out.'

'But you'll need someone else eventually. And some of these people are my friends. They resent the fact I've been brought in as head chef - as *only* chef - and they've basically been booted out.'

'I can't help that. And they haven't been booted out.'

'Their hours have been reduced to nothing. Indefinitely. It's essentially the same. They're not happy. And I don't blame them.'

'I know, I know. I got another text from Jack this morning. The same weird stuff. Something about my promises meaning less than - what was it?' - Davy scrolled through the texts on his phone - '*less than a sugar cube to a luetic dead-end*'. What does that even mean?'

'No idea. I think I can get the gist, though.'

'Why does he have to be so nasty about it, though?'

'You can hardly blame him. You're lucky he hasn't put a brick through the window. Or taken you to court.'

'I did get a couple of letters from ACAS...'

'Fuck's sake, Davy!'

'I just ignored them...'

'*Fuck's sake!* You really are lucky all you're getting is angry texts!'

'I s'pose...'

'No, you really are.'

'Yeah, I guess. Yeah. They're only words, I s'pose. What harm can words do?'

'I dunno, I'd sort it out if I were you.'

*

The barriers were locked when Davy returned to the car park. *What the-?* The barriers were never locked. He had to get a taxi home. There

15

was a gig on at the Arena and it took him an hour and a half. Twenty six quid, it cost him, too.

His eyes hurt too much to turn the lights on when he got home. He ate ready-made chilli straight from the tin in the dark. Foul, it was, barely fit for human consumption, how these people got away with it... But it was sustenance and by that point he didn't care.

He fell into bed with a head like a pressure cooker.

*

He awoke just after five to the cat's mewling.

In the kitchen he found the empty tin of cat food on the draining board, with the fork still in it.

There wasn't another tin of cat food; that was supposed to last a day's meals.

He emptied the tin of chilli into the cat's bowl and went back to bed.

*

Forty minutes later the persistent chirrup of his alarm bored its way into Davy's blockish head like an electronic woodpecker. He sat up woozily. It felt as though some amateur trepanner had taken an ice cream scoop to his brain and emptied a bag of ball-bearings into his skull in its place. He spun about to locate his phone, and the room spun more. And more after that. He stifled the reflex to puke. After almost a minute of spinning this way and that, resulting eventually in his falling off the bed and cracking his head on the still-unused exercise Qube, he finally found it. It was on the small bookcase, under a perfectly rectangular phone-sized hairy mush of chilli-catsick.

*

The shower did not reinvigorate Davy in the way he'd hoped it would. His head still felt like fudge, plus he had a burning sensation down below as if, bluntly - or rather, sharply - put, a javelin had been shoved up his cock and out his arse. Most unpleasant. He waddled, ducklike - no, John Wayne-style - to the mirror to shave, and peered at his reflection. Something was amiss. His mouth seemed puckered, folds and creases furrowing the flesh around his lips like a 60-a-day smoker.

He decided not to shave today.

Must've been an off pint, he thought. Probably a bad reaction, a urinary infection or something.

Still, he'd have to go help in the café, wouldn't he? I mean, the job won't do itself.

*

So that was another fifteen quid on a taxi.

And there was a parking ticket under his windscreen wiper.

Flip it!

*

'Fuck's up with your face?' Olly guffawed when he came in - and up to that point Davy didn't think anybody actually guffawed outside the Beano - 'What's that? Glue steel?'

'Glue-? What?'

'This.' Olly circled his fingers round his lips. 'You look like something out of a Preacher comic.'

'Oh, what!? Is it worse?' Davy slunk into the toilet to check the mirror.

'Depends what you're comparing it to.'

'Ohhhh... My head,' Davy groaned, slumping against the wall, 'feels like a... flipping toothpaste tube.'

'Eh?'

'Like everything's being *squeeeezed* out. I feel like an executive stress ball.' He leant on the baby-change unit, which peremptorily snapped at the hinge and left him crumpled on the tiled floor. Another hundred and fifty quid. And a bruised pelvis. '*Oh-ho-*

17

hohhh!'

    'Go home, man,' Olly said, standing over him, drying his hands with a tea towel, almost avuncular. 'You're not fit to work. You're not well, for fuck's sake.'

    'I have to work,' Davy plainted. 'There's so much to do.'

    'Look at you. You're lying on the toilet floor like a fucking swastika with a face like a bunged-up arse. Go home and go to bed. I'll cope.'

*

Davy did not go home. Davy went to the office. He spent nine hours gazing eyelessly at the middle distance, in which time his lips shrivelled like a salamander on a hotplate. By the time he went home, the lower half of his face looked like that pit with the beastie in it in Star Wars. The upper half felt fit to burst.

And that's not to mention the down below.

*

Davy ran himself a Radox bath -

    - OK, let's be honest, *Radox bath* is a generic term. Davy would have employed nothing in the regime of his toilet as quotidian as Radox. Davy would have had something from at the very least Lush or L'Occitane or some independent artisanal product made by at least three people who sounded like they were born in some quaint little limestone hamlet in the Cotswolds in the 1830s. Puckridge, Bellowlelow & Mellifluous or somesuch. But *Radox bath* fits the bill. So -

    Davy ran himself a *Radox bath* and stripped off all his clothes. Taking a deep breath, he turned and inspected himself in the bathroom mirror. Yep, something was very definitely wrong. His mouth was the most publicly apparent, of course. Olly was right. It did seem - didn't it, he wasn't imagining it? - to resemble... but how, how could it be?... to resemble... it didn't seem possible, but... well, a dilated anus. But

18

what the hell (he allowed himself the profanity in this instance) could've caused that? How does a mouth just - just *transmogrify* itself into a - a sphincter!? And there was more.

His skin too. It seemed smoother, tougher. And drier. Plus it seemed to be cracking in places. Not peeling or flaking, it didn't seem to be just a case of regular old dry skin, or even psoriasis or eczema. It was cracking in a kind of rhomboidal pattern. It wasn't painful or itchy, no, just... well, he wasn't sure. But it was somewhat disconcerting.

And - of course - the down below. Davy didn't even want to look. He had avoided it all day, in fact. He hadn't even gone for a pee at work, out of fear of what he might discover. Of what the guys in the office might discover. Even when he got home, he hadn't looked, he'd simply sat on the toilet and stared at the cabinet. But he was here now, in front of the mirror. He'd have to look. Still he didn't dare. It burned. It burned right through, front to back, as if someone had taken a long, thin, red-hot skewer and inserted it up his urethra and through - taking a bunch of the gubbins down there with it, like a shish kebab - right out through his anus. (His actual anus, that is, not his face-anus. God! imagine that! If he somehow had a face down there now! Or at any rate a mouth. If his mouth and his anus had swapped places. It certainly felt, as the expression goes, as if someone had ripped him a new one.)

He snuck a glance.

As if somehow if he didn't inspect it closely, if he just peeked briefly, it might not prove so bad. It might not be true, whatever it was.

No such luck.

His penis - and don't let's forget the sobriquet - had definitely shrunk. It looked like a timid dormouse poking its nose out of the shrubbery.

Well, that's not good, he thought.

And the back end?

Here goes...

He turned, parted his cheeks, and peered ignominiously through his legs.

A tail!

I've got a flipping tail!

A cluster of haemorrhoids, like a bunch of tiny angry grapes, hung from his anus, fulminating almost audibly.

Oh, Bolsheviks!

Puckridge & Co ain't gonna soothe this away.

*

Brrp! Brrp! Brrp!

Davy slammed the phone into the wall, cracking both the screen and the bedside photo of himself and Connie in the Maldives.

Flip-flippety-ballcocks!

He lay flatly supine on the rumpled bedsheets, feeling like something out of a Beckett play. (He imagined. He'd never actually seen a Beckett play. Not in English anyway. He'd seen *Fin de Partie* with Connie once in Brussels, but his French wasn't sufficiently up to par to follow what was going on. And he wasn't sure he would've known either way. People sitting in bins, moping, who knows...? Still, that's how he felt. Like a mopy bin-man...)

He didn't dare look in the mirror.

*

- Sorry, can't come in today. Splitting headache and feel sick as a dog.

Davy had had to text the office. He couldn't call.

He couldn't speak. He now had a full-blown anus for a mouth. An actual anus. Upon looking in the mirror - a finger-split peek like a teenage girl at the movies - his scream - unlikewise - had come out as a loud wet fart. He'd fainted, fallen onto the toilet, and given himself Armitage Shanks. Unfortunately, he was not in the mood to appreciate the pun. But at least, thanks to his rubbery ring of an arse-mouth, he had not broken a tooth. He was not in the mood to appreciate that either.

'Pprrt-pt-prrrtt!'

A very minced oath.

Now what about the café? Olly couldn't do it on his own. But Davy couldn't serve customers with an arse for a mouth. Imagine the TripAdvisor reviews for that! *Not sure if my cappuccino was being prepared par excellence or if the barista was suffering copious flatulence.* The absolute best he could expect. *The server was an arsehole. Literally.* Hmmm...

Olly would just have to manage.

He needed a doctor.

But what doctor could diagnose this? This wasn't your run-of-the-mill tummy bug or scratchy throat. Ordinary forces were clearly not at play here. He needed someone else.

*

Bzzt!

Another text from Jack. Oh, what now?

- Davy. There's. Still. No. Money. In. My account.

- I'm trying mate, I really am.

- I'll forgo the obvious quip. I don't care how hard you're trying, you're clearly failing. In which case I definitely want my money before the ship goes under.

- I have so much to sort out. I'll definitely get round to you, I promise.

- Promise, my arse! I'm not having you levanting off like some prick out of a Jules Verne novel! You're not weaselling out of this, you c-

Davy clicked the message off. There was no call for language like that! But there was nothing he could do. He'd definitely dug himself in too deep here. I mean, aside from the money, look at the

21

flipping state of him!

The state of the café and his current physical state. Somewhere, somewhere in the back, middle, or frontal lobes of his mind - who knew how these things worked? - Davy had a suspicion that somehow the two were linked. The café's a mess; he's a mess. If he sorts out the café, he should get better. Conversely, if he sorts himself out, the café should pick up. Makes sense. Of course, no practising GP would ever make such a diagnosis. But then Western medical science doesn't know everything, now does it? There are more things in heaven and earth, Horatius, and all that. And he knew a woman - of course he did! - who knew all about various types of holistic therapy. Homeopathy, reiki, *et cetera*. Now some of it was indeed milky pap for credulous nitwits; but *some* of it... Well, exactly. Western medical science doesn't know everything. After all, acupuncture works. And who'd think that? Sticking needles in yourself cures you? Well, that's essentially voodoo. So there's more to some of this stuff than meets the eye.

He decided to give Dizzy a call.

*

Desdemona Wilkes, accredited multidisciplinary holistic therapist and erstwhile svengali, agreed to meet Davy that very morning. Her professional interest was piqued. Davy had only given her a sketchpad outline of the situation, leaving out the more embarrassing details - which is to say, he'd told her practically nothing; after all, it was *all* embarrassing - but Dizzy knew Davy well enough to read between the lines. She promised, both as a professional and a close friend, complete confidentiality, of course, and promised too she would definitely be able to help. She'd been doing this for twenty years, he knew she knew her stuff.

Relief! was Davy's initial response. She was a close friend and a professional. He was in safe hands.

Then he realized he'd have to talk to her.

He'd had to text her before, he couldn't call.

He couldn't speak.

Then he realized when he showed up the situation would pretty much speak for itself.

Still, he couldn't flesh out - an involuntary shudder here - the details. And he could scarcely drop by the Arts Centre and pick up a Sharpie and a stack of idiot boards, not in the shape he was in.

Then he went to the toilet.

And shouted down the pan.

He hadn't meant to.

He had simply been sitting on the toilet, inspecting with growing concern the increasingly lizard-like skin on his arms and legs, when a twist and a push and a shove of his bowels had caused him unconsciously to emit a loud, sonorous grunt into the toilet bowl.

Or rather, not him.

Well, not *him* him...

His anus.

Another push.

It did it again.

Davy paled.

'Fucking hell!' it screamed.

(Potty-mouth.)

Davy slumped face-first onto the carpet, his arse-end burbling away like a drunken jabberwock.

*

He awoke yellow.

On top of everything else, now he was yellow.

Brilliant.

*

He stood before Desdemona's door, bundled, bescarfed, and wrapped like a sherpa despite the unseasonable warmth. He quailed.

Or was that his arse whimpering?

He pressed the doorbell.

Within You, Without You?

She's a professional. And a close friend. It'll be *fine.*

The door slid open like a lover's negligée.

'Well, come in, won't you.'

Too close a friend still. For somebody so spiritual she seemed very much as ever centred on the sensual. That was her spiritual. Still twenty one. Never settled in a relationship, never had a proper job.

No, no. She's a professional.

Davy squeezed himself between her sinuous black-clad frame and the wall, and crept down the hall.

'Nice get-up,' she called after him. 'Are you trying to get yourself arrested?'

Davy let out a small fart and half-waved apologetically by way of response. He made his way to the living room. She followed close behind, and bade him sit on the capacious leather sofa. He duly sat, and sank six inches, his knees practically on par with his ears.

'So what exactly is it?' she queried with a wry curl of her purple-painted lips, pouring Davy the thimbliest of oolong teas. 'You were very nonspecific. Although I assume it has something to do with why you're all done up like Tintin in Tibet.'

Davy pointed to his mouth beneath his ski mask as he fought his way out of the sandtrap of a sofa. He disrobed himself of his Lowe Alpine Roald Amundsen jacket, and started removing his hat, mask, and shades.

'Look at all this,' she was saying; 'it can't be - *Jesus Christ! You're yellow!'*

He tried to make himself as small and innocuous as he could as she examined him like a lab specimen.

'And *scaly.*'

She peered at his face closely. *Very* closely.

'And what the fuck's happened here? You look like a hagfish or something.'

This, this was the worst part. This was the bit he'd dreaded.

He scrambled to drag himself out of his leathery oubliette.

'Can you even speak through that?'

This was it.

The ignominy.

The Ignominy.

Capitalized. *Italicized.*

He stood up, pulled down his jeans and pants - her eyebrows arched already at his pygostyle of a penis - and turned to face her. Well, to arse-face her.

'Sorry,' he squeaked.

If he'd farted nitrous oxide she couldn't have laughed more.

Ordinarily Davy's face would've ruddied like a sunblush tomato. But lizards don't blush.

'Oh my God!' she howled. 'What the fuck've you done?'

'I don't know.'

'You've got a tail of piles! And your cock's gone!'

'I am aware of that.'

'You've got an arse for a mouth! And you're... reptilian.'

'Yeah, that hadn't escaped my notice either.'

'And you - sorry, but... - talk through your arse. What the fuck did you do?'

'I think it might be linked to the café.'

'It's not going so well?'

She'd calmed a little; it was the first note of genuine solicitude in her voice. Of course. She loved the café. Never mind me! Davy thought. So long as nothing happens to the café! He tried to remember she was a professional. A professional who laughed in his face - well, his arse - but still a professional.

'I've pissed quite a few people off, I think.'

'You think it might be karmic?'

'I suppose you could say I've been a... a bit of an arsehole.'

Dizzy lifted the pile-tail and poked gently at the arse-mouth. 'What d'you think?' it said.

Like something you'd definitely call a plumber out for.

'I think you need to try to make some reparations,' she suggested, lighting a cigarette and settling back in her chair.

'You think that'll help?' he parped.

'Can't hurt.'

She smiled a *schadenfreudoh* smile. It *was* pretty funny, in its way. Bless him, he *was* a bit of an arse.

'All I'd say at this stage is it's a good job you weren't a complete cunt.'

... and now he thinks he can just get away with it all by paying me the money he owes me and I won't publish - as he doubtless would maintain, the little skink! - flagrant untruths and scurrilous libel? By turning around now and doing The Decent Thing? Oh no, you don't get away with it that easily, my friend!

No. Publish and be damned.

To be continued...?

Of Maccydee's and Not-So-Much Men

Meredith Blanchwater

So that was my choice.

Food and a bus home. Or the book.

It may be no choice at all for you. A book? You're hungry, yet you'd forego lunch and walk several miles home just to buy a book? Not even a rare book.

No, not even a rare book. *Of Mice And Men.* Paperback. But I only have a fiver.

The book is £4.99.

So it's either the book, or it's McDonald's and a bus ticket.

I can't have both.

And I really want the book.

But I am really hungry. And I'd rather not walk, especially not hungry, all the way home.

I know what the sensible thing to do would be.

But I really want the book.

I *really* want the book.

I *need* the book.

And as I glance from the serge blue of its cover to the golden arches out across the road, I notice there's nobody else on this aisle. I straighten, and make a quick furtive recce of the bookshop; but casually, as if unkinking a crick in my neck.

There may be a way I can have both.

I had always loved books. I had always loved reading. I do not remember, it is a long time ago now, but I think my mother taught me to read before I went to school. And she had intended to send me to the school down the hill. It had a good reputation. Or so I believe. I do not remember. But the school were outraged I could already read. That

29

is not how we do things here, they said. She will have to learn again.

My mother, quite rightly, thought this ludicrous.

So I went to the school round the corner. I do not remember much of this either. But I do remember having my pick of any book at the book fair, to be paid for by the school bully after an incident that landed me in A&E. I picked a guide to prehistoric animals. To my credit, I thought, it was also one one the cheaper books in the fair.

But then I also tricked him into looking at the toes on my snowman and kicked him in the head. Nobody believed him.

None of this really matters. We moved away not long after.

We moved to another small town. Another small town with another small school. I still loved reading. I still loved words. I was fortunate - I now realize - that it came to me like falling off a climbing frame. We now had spelling tests; but words held no terror for me. Not for me the swirling jumble of letters the not-so-bright Dorothys of the class seemed caught up in. For me, the spelling tests - and I assume they were tests; I assume they gave us chance to revise, again I don't remember - well, I literally just sat down and practised writing out whatever words the teacher read out in as fancy or ridiculous writing as I felt like that afternoon. Or morning. Or whenever it was...

I'd soon read all the books in the library, including an encyclopaedia of human biology. It was not comprehensive in its detail, it was no *Gray's Anatomy*, but I knew how that great intrigue Sex worked before any of my counterparts, even in the year above. (Biologically-speaking, of course. It was also no *Kama Sutra*. But that was a way off yet...) Oh, I could have shown off with my knowledge; but it was so much more fun to hold my tongue and smirk inwardly at their misguided, misinformed, misinterpreted, and misbegotten little romances.

Smart, maybe; noble, no.

But I think we've already established virtue was already not necessarily one of my strong points. Faith, Hope, and Charity? Why, yes. They were in my class, I knew them well. Who did you think I was laughing at?

And so, having picked this carcass clean, I moved up to middle school.

It was a shock.

I was disciplined on the first day for calling one of the boys a twat.

Now let me explain this...

A teacher had overheard me in the schoolyard, and taken me to one side.

Do you know what a twat is? she had said.

Yes, I had replied. I did. I had accidentally called my mother a twat a couple of years previously, conflating the word with twit. It had not gone down well. That is not a nice word! she had 'explained', without telling me what it meant. So of course I had gone and looked it up. All its meanings. OK, I had not meant to call my mother a twat.

I had definitely meant to call this boy a twat, however. So:

Yes, I do.

There's absolutely no need for such language!

He pushed me into a wall for no reason! I countered.

But some people find that word very offensive!

Well, good, that's how it was meant. He's a twat.

But you could've used another word, though!

I could, but I probably still would have sworn.

She stared at me, her face almost immobile, but the tiniest of tics here and there - about the eyes, about the nostrils, about the corners of the lips - betraying something I seemed to be on the edge of wondering if I thought I comprehended. I said nothing, stood like a statue, *my* expression motionless. And then:

Go on, get out of here! And no more swearing!

I think I also expected the world to have moved on, as it were. No. We were still reading the same old texts. In the advanced set, we'd started on Roald Dahl and CS Lewis. Great books, but... I'd already read them. Them and *The Lord of the Rings* and Ursula Le Guin and Asimov and *The Origin of Species* and countless National Geographics. Now I was, what? ten years old and I'm not saying by any stretch of the imagination that I fully comprehended all these books, but I had read them. Something had filtered through. It might fairly and still in all modesty be said I was reading beyond my years. But personally I'd still maintain ten is late to be *starting* on Dahl and Lewis.

I think this was most forcibly, or at any rate laboriously, brought home to me when Miss Copydex read to the class *The Hobbit.*

An aside. In my second year at middle school my class teacher was a woolly, bespectacled bundle of ineptitude by the name of Miss Cosway. She was, frankly, a terrible teacher. Even at ten I knew this. But, being ten, was not sure if what I knew, or what I thought I knew, was necessarily true, or correct. The world of adults was confusing, and much of it was never explained. Or it was *explained away* with the old catch-all: *You'll understand when you're older.* I may be missing something. But when my mother came home from a parents' evening in a purple fury after being told that my work was 'good in general, but she has no imagination', she told me: 'That woman is an idiot. I wouldn't listen to a word she says. How she's a teacher I'll never know.' So I was right. Miss Cosway was useless.

Which brings us onto Copydex. Well, one day, just after lunch break, as she was about to commence afternoon register, Miss Cosway somehow contrived to spill a whole bottle of Copydex - you know, that horrible fish-glue stuff - all down her cashmere jumper. She was distraught, to say the least. And who wouldn't be? It is horrible stuff, it stinks, and cashmere is expensive. She'd have to wash it off immediately or the jumper would be ruined, if it wasn't already. At which point she took the unprecedented decision to leave the entire class unattended - and unregistered - and drive home to wash her top and change. The class predictably ran riot. I'd like to say I simply sat quietly and read my book. But come on - I was ten.

Now the school was open-plan, there were no doors, so when half an hour later the deputy head walked past our classroom and witnessed the pandemonium within, well, he went off like Krakatoa and took out about two dozen ceiling tiles. *Wild?* as the Not The Nine O'Clock News sketch goes; *he was livid.*

And she didn't return for a further hour.

How she remained with her job intact is a miracle. But hence the nickname Miss Copydex. So Miss Copydex was reading us *The Hobbit*, in uninspiring monotone. Now it's a wonderful piece of fantasy, arguably the birth of the fantasy genre as we know it today, and kids love it. But read like a Sunday school sermon? The whole class was bored to the point of stupor. And as I sat there, rolling and unrolling and rolling and unrolling and rolling and unrolling my tie, I thought: *What am I doing here, wasting my time? Where am I going? What am I learning that I don't already know, that I haven't already read, that I couldn't just find in a book anyway?*

Miss Copydex droned on, like a drowsy bumblebee: *'Sssss'* *said Gollum, and became quite polite. 'Praps ye sits here and chats with it a bitsy, my preciousss.'* Like the understudy to the serpent in the Garden of Eden; that is if he were half-drunk and the prospect of original sin bored him witless.

And *this* is supposed to be fun. *This* is supposed to be a break from the lessons. *This* is where we get to loose our imaginations. Everyone's half-asleep!

This is bollocks!

To cut a long story short, I must have said something to that effect when I went home. Anyway, not long after I found myself sitting entrance exams for local grammar schools.

I got in. To all of them. The best one, though - supposedly, at least according to my parents, and the school itself (Duncan Goodhew practised in this pool, they said) - terrified me. It was like a prison. Long, narrow, tiny-windowed corridors, and all painted grey. Plus pupils had to come in on Saturday mornings. True, they got Wednesday afternoons off, but that seemed scant recompense to my mind. I went for the second best. Won an assisted place, in fact, otherwise my parents would never have been able to afford to send me.

Now this was more like a place of learning. It was old. Founded in 1612 (Joseph Priestley was an alumnus), although the present building was not that old. The oldest part of the school though was the library. A huge library; at least compared to the single - though at the time hallowed - carpeted square surrounded like some papier-mâché and sticky-back-plastic Rome by seven precarious bookshelves that was my middle school library. A huge old library of wood and a billion pages. Shelf after shelf of books on every subject. Algebra to Zarathustra. It smelt beetly and bready. Farinaceous with the dusting of words.

Now I was at home.

So this is where you find me.

Not right now. Right now you find me in WHSmith, attempting to half-inch a Steinbeck. We'll come back to that.

In general, though; here. Here in this library. At lunchtimes or skiving Games or PE. Somewhere towards the back, beyond the reach of the radar gaze of the glassy librarian, who has the look of an owl but the *look* of a basilisk. The desks all have a wooden backboard with an ancillary shelf, kind of like a Welsh dresser, so they're easy to hide behind. Easy to hide behind, easy to steal books behind. Of course all books should be signed out, but how're they going to know? One, two, three books in my bag, *alley-oop!* and up to the desk to sign out the fourth. And out we go, no one the wiser. Nobody reads these books anyway. They don't care, they're not interested, they're none of them here to learn. It's much like middle school in that respect, except these kids are richer. *I'll* actually read this. I'll love it and give it a good home.

I need these books. I'm going to be a great writer.

Over the past five years I have managed to *reappropriate* probably half the output of Penguin Classics, including chunks of Kafka, Gogol, Gorky, Dostoyevsky, Chekhov, Pushkin, and Bulgakov. And, fittingly, *The Communist Manifesto* and *The Ragged-Trousered Philanthropists*. Plus *A Brief History of Time, Surely You're Joking, Mr Feynman?*, a brand-new copy of *The Quark and the Jaguar*, and a hundred-year-old edition of *The Origin of Species*. Likewise Haldane, Dawkins, Dennett, and a number of anthologies of essays by Stephen Jay Gould. Who turned me on to Twain. And Bierce and James and Faulkner and Steinbeck and Hemingway and -

'Hemingway?' murmured Joanne Tomlinson. Like a dove. 'You're usually reading the Russian authors, aren't you?'

'I... um...' I flapped like a fish literally out of water. *Joanne Tomlinson.* 'I... I read all sorts.'

'We-ell,' - she ran on Castrol GTX or something - 'if you're out of the great grey Slavic shadow you might want to try Steinbeck.'

'I... intend to.' I did. And indeed I had read an excerpt from *Log from The Sea of Cortez* in Gould. But that wasn't gonna wash. Plus I couldn't say I'd nicked *Travels with Charley* but not read it yet.

'*Cannery Row* is a good place to start.' She leant against my desk like a dream. 'Joyous. It's like sunbathing in the nude.'

If I hadn't read Feynman *et al.* I would've sworn I was a puddle of quicksilver on the library carpet.

'I.. I..' I burbled, 'I will.'

'Cool, have fun. See you.'

And she glided away like Ariel into the ether.

Joanne Tomlinson.

Reader, I married her.

God! how I would love to speak those words.

Yes, it would seem I was sapphic.

Nowadays, of course, whether I preferred girls or boys would cause no more consternation than if I were to say I voted Labour or Tory. Probably less, in fact. But remember this was 1995. It doesn't feel that long ago but it was a different age. I would've been largely accepted, no doubt - No Doubt: God, how I fancied Gwen Stefani too! - but social mores were still in retrospect practically Neanderthal. And that's giving bad press to Neanderthals. What with Britpop and the burgeoning Lad culture - I'm not saying the one necessarily led to the other, correlation is not causation after all, but the two did pretty much go hand-in-hand, it seemed; and listen to Blur's *Girls And Boys* now, it's a simple-minded affair, isn't it, really? - my sexuality would've still been something stigmatized, something at once praised and patronized. A year or so later of course there would be Girl Power. And again I would hasten to comment that I'm not saying that didn't work or didn't have any effect, but look how that was treated at the time too, and look how time has treated it since.

So anyway, as Blur - whom I love, incidentally; they had far more range than Oasis - sang: *Love in the nineties / Is paranoid.* I told nobody. I swooned over Joanne Tomlinson. Swooned and masturbated. I dreamt of her. At night, in the morning, on the bus, in the library. Dreams of 'stolen moments' in some secluded wooded tract of the weekly cross-country run, as if in the mud of Gethsemane, where Siegfried and Wilfred lost mind and life. I wrote yearning, tragic poems - you can tell, can't you - and drew countless pictures, and even wrote her name on the inside covers of my folders and exercise books. I know. So cliché. But at the time... Oh, just to write her name, to draw her face, her neck, the fold and flick of her hair...

But she was way out of my league. If we were even playing the same game. I mean, she didn't hang out with the likes of me. She was as distant, mysterious, and unattainable as some Vedic deity.

How could I even speak to her? The likes of me? I couldn't, could I.

But *she* had spoken to me.

A few words only. But even so...

And she had noticed what I was reading.

True, Jimmy Bridger had also noticed me reading a Penguin 60s edition of *The Man That Corrupted Hadleyburg*, and I didn't assume he was interested in me in that way. At least I hoped not. *Ugh!* There was the lumpen proletariat right there!

No, this was different, I convinced myself.

Or tried to convince myself.

Hoped.

Dreamt.

This was different.

For maybe a week - *maybe!* she says, as if she wasn't counting every delicious tortured minute of it; as if she wasn't totting up the hours she hadn't acted on her impulse, totting up the hours she was sitting feet away, totting up the hours she had scoured the shelves for more Steinbeck - What kind of a library is this!? - totting up the hours she had said, she had snarled, she had *screamed through her soul she could bear it no longer!...*

I had screamed the silentest scream...

For maybe a week - seven days to the day - I scarcely slept but without slipping into an almost fevered delirium of limbs as pale and smooth and cool as alabaster; hair like some exotic melting moss hung from slender, sorrowful cypresses; nails like the talons of some gentle favoured falcon...

Lips like...

Lips like sugar.

Echo & the Bunnymen, on a private perpetual reel in the soft crepuscular purgatory of my mind.

So here I am. No great leap of the imagination.

Here I am, and this is my choice.

Food and a bus home. Or the book.

No, it's not *Cannery Row*. They don't have *Cannery Row*. But it is Steinbeck.

It is Steinbeck.

It's a pass.

A *passepartout,* I hope.

I'm reading Steinbeck...

Then the alabaster limbs and the lips like sugar...

I clock the salient compass-points of the shop, still fingering the book in my sweating palms.

This is no school library.

No excuses, no leniency here.

This is theft, no two ways about it.

I hesitate - probably too long, don't I always? - and without even breathing make my play. I slip the book under my jacket and head for the door.

A tall man with a tie moves. A deliberate move and considered, though he's no knight.

And another, and he no rook.

Two of them.

I'm outmanoeuvred.

I change tack and head to the cash register. Insouciantly, slipping the book back into my hand, as if that was my intention all along.

I hand over my fiver without any show of equivocation.

A large hand falls on my shoulder.

'A word, please...'

A word.

Another word.

These words will be my undoing.

I'm frogmarched into an office, feeling - and this is a hark back now - like Josef K.

The room is small.

Of course.

So the words can expand and fill it to its very corners, like foam on the first sputterings of a volatile fire.

I step out into the street, shamefaced even though no one knows my would-be crime.

It's going to be a long, cold, hungry walk.

And not the last, I feel.

No. I feel I will be walking alone, cold and hungry, all my life.

How To Drown While Wearing A Life Vest

Barry Marshall

Lucy sat on the garden swing, as instructed, and watched Dan-Dad's pale reflection in the greenhouse as he tinkered with the car and popped in and out of the house. Lucy shivered with anticipation. She liked watching him do normal, everyday things when she knew he could not see her. There was something enjoyable, something secretive about it. What was one more tiny secret these days?

Lucy had called him Dan-Dad for as long as she had known him. She was not going to stop now, even if it was only in her head. She knew that Dan-Dad used to like his nickname. He probably still did, though it only made him look sad when she would say it, or *sadder* than usual. Instead, she kept Dan-Dad at the back of her tongue where she could not say the thing that would make him both happy and unhappy. She heard grown-ups call this a quandary, which was a word her tongue liked the feel of, even if her brain did not really get what it meant. He never called her Spindleshanks or Hobgoblin anymore either, despite the fact that Lucy saw his lips go to shape the words before he caught himself. She supposed a draw was only fair.

The shiver turned into a full-blown shudder. The sun was still waking itself up and the summer air felt freezy cold. The grass was dark grey in the shadows and damp with dew. Lucy rubbed her goosebumpy arms and willed Dan-Dad to take shorter, quicker strides.

'Psst. What you up to, Lucy-Lu?'

Sammy Next-Door stood with her cheeks bulgy with bubblegum, resting her chin on the garden fence and *existing with the sunrise* as usual… whatever that meant. Even at this early hour her face looked greasy and grubby.

Dan-Dad's reflection in the dim glass window bowed its head and traipsed into the house. She hopped off the swing and pulled a cinder block over to the fence so that she was close to eye level with Sammy Next-Door. Sammy was rather small for twelve, and Lucy was sure that she would be much taller when she got to her age.

'Spying,' said Lucy. 'Are you making a meeting?'

'*Calling* a meeting, you infant,' said Sammy. 'No, just wondering why you're up so early. What's in there?'

'Nothing!' Lucy glanced behind her at the rucksack in case the contents suddenly grew legs and ran back into the house where they came from. 'I'm going on a road-trip.'

'Hmm,' said Sammy. 'You do well for a ginger step-child. "Specially one as daft and lanky as you, lame-o.'

Lucy laughed hard, making the entire cinder block wobble. She knew Sammy Next-Door would always be on her team. A good friend who cared about her and talked to her as if nothing had happened. The only one who treated Lucy like she was made of flesh and bone, rather than glass.

'It's supposed to be a surprise but I heard him talking on the phone to Auntie Kim again. We're going over the border to her house.'

'He's phoning her a lot,' said Sammy. She waggled her eyebrows. 'Maybe he wants something more than just a visit.'

Lucy thought about this for a moment before the penny dropped. 'Eww, don't be weird. That's my auntie!'

'I didn't even know your Mam had a sister until... you know,' said Sammy. She looked thoughtful. 'Sorry, it's just a bit out of the blue, that's all.'

'I've only met her twice and once was...' Lucy sucked in the cold air. She shook her head and let her breath mist out. 'I can't hear everything they say,' she continued, 'but they talk about me all the time, so they're treating me. A day out or something.'

Sammy peered at Dan-Dad.

'He looks like he needs a day out. Guy's turning into a zombie.'

Lucy said nothing. She felt tired too, with all the late-night eavesdropping. She did not feel bad about it, though. Hearing people talk about her felt like a big glass of chocolate milk. She could not remember the last time Dan-Dad bought regular milk.

'Anyway,' Lucy said. 'What are you doing today?'

'Nothing,' said Sammy. 'Sick of YouTube. Can't wait for the holidays to be over. Well, Dan's staring into space again. You'd better put a leash on him before he wanders off.'

Lucy craned her neck. Dan-Dad was resting his arm on the car roof and, yes, staring into space.

'He does that,' she said. 'He's probably ready to go.'

Sammy Next-Door wondered about this for a second. Then, like a viper in dungarees, she reached over the fence to fling two arms around Lucy's neck in a squashy hug. She pulled away just as quickly. 'Smell you later, Lucy-Lu,' said Sammy, turning away.

'I'll smell you first,' said Lucy. She felt slightly dazed by the hug.

Sammy ambled back towards her decking and sat with her back to Lucy, stretching out her legs to catch the first rays of sunlight as they began to creep out from behind the houses.

Lucy hopped off the cinder block and skipped back towards the swing, unzipping her rucksack to double-check that she had everything she needed. She re-tied her laces, straightened her jeans and, drawing a blank for other reasons to delay, went to join Dan-Dad at the car.

The silence in the car was that weird kind of silence, the words like crocodiles lurking beneath the surface of the swamp. Lucy did not expect them to snap or bite, but it was impossible to pretend that they were not there. She occupied herself by kicking her feet against the bottom of the glovebox, hoping that Dan-Dad would tell her to stop it. When that failed, she hummed and played I-Spy by herself until she felt too silly to continue. How much easier it would be to have gotten the coach alone to Auntie Kim's, or sprouted wings and flown there by herself. One was no lonelier a number than two.

Out of the corner of her eye, Lucy saw Dan-Dad's head slowly roll in her direction, then flick back as she glanced up at him. He looked tired. He always looked tired, but he looked *extra* tired this time. He had been driving for ages. The car was hot and Lucy wished he would put the windows down. Frankly, he stunk today. There was no point in asking. The sky was still cloudy, so the answer would be a firm *no*.

Lucy felt bad for him and mad at herself. This was Dan-Dad's road-trip too. The least she could do was treat him to a conversation.

'Are we nearly there yet?' she said, letting her voice trill in the hope of a *yuk-yuk* laugh.

Dan-Dad stared straight ahead at the road.

'Not for a bit,' he said.

This was the most he had said for yonks. Once, he would have told her it would be ten minutes, then fifty years the next time she asked, then a squillion seconds if Lucy could count that high. She thought it would be pointless to try and bring that routine back from the dead. At least these were real words that he had uttered, rather than a grunt or sigh, so she was satisfied with it for now.

She picked at a scab on her knee, watching the blood ooze up before wiping it with her thumb and onto the seat. That, too, went unnoticed. Lucy's Mam would have spied this straight away. She would have yelled in horror and poured her handbag onto her own lap in search of a plaster, all while Dan-Dad would roll his eyes and try not to grin.

She pushed the image away by counting her freckles. When she lost count, Lucy played Yellow Car by herself until a road-sign caught her eye.

'It's only twenty miles until Seahouses,' she shouted. 'Is that by the beach?'

Dan-Dad mulled the question over.

'The name would suggest so,' he said eventually.

'Can we go? Have we got time for the beach?'

A long pause.

'Did you put a swimming suit in your bag?'

Lucy's hand flung out at the rucksack before her, pausing with her thumb and forefinger holding the zip. She thought better than to let Dan-Dad see inside.

'I didn't think of that,' she said. 'But there must be shops. If there's houses, there'll be shops.' Lucy beamed at how rock solid her own logic was, then worried about the depth of Dan-Dad's wallet with him not working these days. 'If you've got money, I mean. It's ok if you don't.'

She watched Dan-Dad carefully. He had always looked thirties-old, but now he looked old-old. Lucy missed his squishy hugs less now that Dan-Dad had grown his beard so long. When he had married her Mam, he always had rough, spiky hair on his chin that rubbed her cheek red whenever she gave out her goodnights, but Lucy thought of these stingy patches as a rash of love. She did not want to be tickled by this bushy eyesore, though. It still had toast crumbs in it most of the time.

Just when Lucy wondered whether Dan-Dad had either missed the question or refused to answer, he turned his head to shoot her a quick look that her Mam had always called his *appraising expression.* His eyes looked huge and empty behind his glasses, the blue seeming to fade to a duller grey every day.

'We can go to the beach,' he said. 'It's not a problem.'

'High five,' shouted Lucy, but Dan-Dad left her hanging. To be fair, he had both hands on the wheel. 'Why is it called Seahouses?' she asked. 'Are they houses in the sea, like on stilts? Is it just the sailors who live there?'

'I don't think so.'

'Do you think they're like regular houses, or different somehow?'

Dan-Dad paused.

'Some people think a house is a home, but they're different concepts. A house is always regular, a home is something more fluid. Sometimes you can control a fluid but other times it runs through your fingers and you don't know how to stop it.'

Lucy gazed at him, her heart feeling swollen against her breastbone. This was more like the old him; the professor. He always laughed as Lucy tried to unpick the puzzle in his riddles. When she was little, she had always imagined a professor to be an old geezer with fluffy white hair and goggles, frantically pouring beakers into test-tubes. Dan-Dad was not a mad scientist, he was just a normal guy who would play horsies with her and set impossible riddles for her to decode, laughed with her but never at her. There was a difference between the two, she knew that much.

Lucy thought about the fluid. Her mind showed her no pictures that were especially helpful, only various shades of blue.

'I wonder what colour the houses are,' she said, feeling that this was the key to the puzzle. She snapped her fingers in triumph. 'Sea. Houses. They have to be blue... right?'

Pause.

'I'm not sure. I've never been there.'

'Did you never stop there with Mam on the way to Auntie Kim's before?'

Another pause stretching out for *aaaages.*

'I've never been to Auntie Kim's before either.'

'Oh.'

Lucy knew that her Mam and auntie never really talked to each other much. She made sure to keep an eye on Auntie Kim at the church to make sure that she was nice to Dan-Dad, who still answered to the name at that point. The grown-ups smiled at each other, but Lucy knew that neither of them wanted to. She bet *they* knew that the other knew that. At first, Lucy felt jealous of how good most grown-ups were at pretending, then dreaded ever becoming one. If grown-ups were so good at pretending then how did they know when they were really happy?

'Are you hungry?' said Dan-Dad suddenly. 'I'm sorry, I didn't realise the time. You must be starving.'

'I'm ok,' said Lucy instantly. She wanted to save the money for the possible swimming costume. She looked at Dan-Dad's thin wrists and thought better of it. 'I'll have something to eat if you're hungry though.'

'I can get your swimsuit as well. Maybe a beach towel and a ball if that's what you want, or we could have a picnic on the beach, yeah?'

Lucy waited to see if the babble of words had exhausted themselves. Dan-Dad's eyes were hopping like tiny sparrows from the road to her and back again. The corners of his mouth were trying to remember the journey from a straight line to an upwards arch. His knuckles were white against the wheel.

'Come on,' said Dan-Dad. 'You can have as much as you want.'

Lucy's memory flashed up the Christmas of a couple of years ago. She fought so hard to make the night last forever that she ended up rolling around the floor and kicking her legs, before Dan-Dad had to physically carry her to bed because she would not get off the floor. Why did his face now remind her of that night?

Lucy hugged her arms against the icy coldness in her stomach.

'I could eat a burger,' she said.

For a short while, Lucy counted the passing road-signs until she saw the familiar yellow arches swing into view. She dawdled, picking the rucksack up from between her legs and putting it on her knee as Dan-Dad pulled the car in-between two others.

'You can just leave that here, you know. No sense in lugging it about.'

Lucy dug her fingers into the fabric. What if someone stole it? What if he needed something from the car when they were inside the restaurant, and decided to check that she had everything?

'Can I put it in the boot?' Lucy asked.

A funny look passed over Dan-Dad's face and the light went out of his eyes again.

'The boot is full,' he mumbled.

Lucy could not remember him packing any luggage, but then she could not see from the garden swing, nor in the reflection from the dingy window of the greenhouse.

'Please?'

Dan-Dad promised that he would check and got out to rummage in the boot for space. While the back window was blocked, Lucy quickly snatched the book out of the bag and put it in the glovebox. Once slapping the door shut, she climbed off her seat and shrugged at Dan-Dad.

'It'll be ok on the floor, I guess,' she said, walking past him and up the steps of the entrance.

His shoulders slumped and he silently followed Lucy into the restaurant.

Dan-Dad picked at his burger while Lucy demolished hers. She watched him gulp down the rest of his drink and he let out a wet, raggy burp without noticing. Lucy giggled and put out her palm but Dan-Dad was off exploring his own head again. This time, being left hanging felt more insulting. He really had no excuse. Lucy gritted her teeth and dug in the meal box for the free toy, a purple and blue fluffy kitty.

'Does Auntie Kim have a cat?' she asked.

'A cat?' said Dan-Dad. 'I don't know. Why?'

'I like cats. I think I'd quite like a kitty.'

'At Kim's?'

'No, silly,' said Lucy. 'At home. I asked you for one ages ago, remember?'

'Doesn't it seem odd to you that big hairless apes invite tiny panthers into their homes, knowing that they could never possibly communicate with each other?'

'Does it seem odd to you?'

Dan-Dad leaned forward in his seat.

'It never used to, but now I think it *is* bizarre. Maybe the panther gets frustrated at the ape not being able to teach it anything useful and it would prefer to go back to the jungle. What do you think? Is the ape being selfish?'

Lucy thought hard about the question. She rubbed her collar-bone, where Sammy Next-Door was bound to have left a bruise.

'It's not selfish and you don't need to speak cat to talk to it,' she said. 'Sometimes hugs are enough.'

Dan-Dad looked at his uneaten chips.

'I should've gotten chicken,' he said in a weird, squeaky voice and then made a show of turning around in his seat to look at the menu.

Lucy left it at that. He got like this sometimes and making a fuss of him only made it worse. One thing was for sure: she was not getting a cat any time soon.

Lucy gazed across the madhouse of a restaurant at the table of kids sitting and playing on tablets, ignoring their food. An angry mother wagged her finger in the face of a curly haired boy who was amusing himself by bopping his little sister with a balloon.

'Hey,' said Lucy, poking Dan-Dad's elbow. 'I never got a balloon.'

Dan-Dad turned back to her, his eyes red and sore-looking.

'What?'

'A balloon. I never got one. Can you ask for one at the counter?'

'Why don't you get an ice cream or something? I said you could have whatever you wanted.'

'I want a balloon.'

'You're eight,' said Dan-Dad. 'Aren't you too old for balloons now?'

'You're never too old for balloons. Will you just get one?' Lucy said, feeling her bottom lip quiver.

'Of all the pointless things I can think of, a balloon is the absolute zenith.'

Lucy did not know what a zenith was and did not care. She just wanted a balloon.

'You're being mean,' she said. She could tell he knew that, too, but he was too far gone to stop.

'Look Lucy, I'm sorry,' he said in a low voice. 'But I don't think I'm really getting this. A balloon is all well and good in principle, but as soon as you get one you end up damaging it. The longer you have it, the more you push it out of shape, and you lose what makes it so pretty in the first place. Sometimes, Lucy, if you want to see how high a balloon can float, you have to let go of it. So, what's the point?'

Lucy folded her arms across her chest.

'Nobody wants a balloon just to look at it or make it float. It does that on its own anyway. You're supposed to play with it, make it fart and stuff. Did you learn anything from having a kid?'

'Yes,' snapped Dan-Dad. 'I learned how to drown while wearing a life-vest.'

'Just stop it,' said Lucy. 'Stop talking in riddles all the time. That one doesn't even make sense. Life-vests float just as well as balloons do.'

Lucy glared at Dan-Dad and she felt her heart crawl around in her chest as he covered his face with both hands. One or both of them had gone too far and she had no idea which. Maybe she was wrong. Maybe life-vests didn't float as well as balloons did, but it was nothing to get upset over.

'Life-vests,' muttered Dan-Dad into his hands. He looked up and smiled at Lucy, his real smile. 'Come on, I don't want to sit here squabbling. I want to have a nice time before we see Auntie Kim. Grab your things, we're going to the beach while the sun's out.'

Lucy nodded. She had thought about marching over to the counter and grabbing a balloon on the way out, or wrestling the curly haired boy for his, but she did not want Dan-Dad to see that, even though her anger would certainly excuse her. She was already grown-up enough to know that neither of them had won the argument. She would have to be grown-up and bury the disagreement next to the hurt she still felt.

They went over a humpy road fast enough for Lucy's stomach to follow a second behind her on the way down. Dan-Dad broke into a grin at Lucy's squeals, though his face seemed to be trying to tell his mouth not to. They pulled into the little town or village (the difference between the two was a total mystery) and searched for a parking spot. Dan-Dad lurked like a beardy vulture next to the mini golf course until another driver pulled out.

Lucy bounded out of the car and wrenched Dan-Dad by the hand towards the ancient-looking shop opposite. Amongst all the cool little knick-knacks she found a bright, blue, one-piece swim-suit. She had her eye on a seashell picture frame too, but did not want to push her luck. Aside from anything else, it did not seem to have dawned on Dan-Dad yet that he would have to hold the towel around Lucy while she changed into it on the beach. The crimson blush would be worth a few pounds in itself.

Dan-Dad refused the offer of a plastic bag because it was more important to help save the polar bears, so Lucy took off her bag while he bought some chips for the long, long walk to the dunes. It was then that she realised the book was still in the glovebox.

'We have to go back to the car,' she said.

Dan-Dad scoffed a chip. 'Why?'

'I've forgotten something.'

Dan-Dad looked at the rucksack curiously.

'What?'

Lucy fidgeted from one foot to the other.

'I don't know.'

'How do you know you've forgotten something if you don't know what it is?'

Lucy could almost feel the cogs grinding in her head.

'Changed,' she mumbled.

'Come again?'

'I have to get changed,' she half-shouted. 'If I don't go back and get changed in the car, you'll have to cover me up with a towel.'

'Oh right,' said Dan-Dad. His face fell, the blush appearing several shades lighter than Lucy had hoped for. 'I really should have thought about that. Sorry, Lucy, I'm a total…'

Lucy felt dismayed at the darkening of his face, the scolding he was giving himself deep inside.

'It's ok,' she said. 'You bought a massive big towel. It'll do.'

'A woodsman worth his salt counts trees, not forests,' he said, still lost in his own thoughts.

Please, Lucy thought, no more riddles. She took Dan-Dad's hand and pulled him through the long grass around the dunes and towards the sandy cove. The water looked like a sheet of glittery stars under the afternoon sun. The sand was studded with people playing football, lounging under the hot sun, digging holes and throwing balls for their dogs to chase into the surf. Lucy hoped the last part would cheer Dan-Dad up more than anything else. She could bear the loss of her potential kitty more easily now that she remembered the way Dan-Dad always rolled around on the floor with stranger's dogs in the park. He must have never been a cat person. Dan-Dad looked away as he held the towel around Lucy. She wriggled out of her jeans and top and into the swimmers as quickly as she could.

'There,' she said. 'I'm already finished and you did a good job of covering me.'

Dan-Dad looked at her blankly before a small smile crept over his mouth.

'You've taught me something new, then,' he said.

'I wish it was how to play video games, but it's a start,' Lucy nodded, hard enough for her pigtails to flail about.

Dan-Dad laughed then looked sad about laughing in that way that he did now. He flapped out the towel and beckoned her to sit next to him.

'I should be the one teaching you things, I believe,' he said.

'But you *do*. You give me riddles all the time.'

'Mmm. I'm not sure that's as helpful as I tell myself it is, Hobgoblin.'

'I get them sometimes,' said Lucy, before she realised what he had called her. Her eyes instantly swam. 'I got the ape and panther one. That one was a breeze, Dan-Dad.'

They sat quietly in the hot glare of the sun as Dan-Dad rubbed his mouth for a while.

'I should be honest with you, I guess,' he said. 'I don't think getting a cat is a good idea.'

'I know,' said Lucy, excited at getting there before the professor for once. 'I got that ages ago, too. Look, there's a spaniel over there, shall I call it over?'

Dan-Dad glanced at the dog and rubbed his temple.

'You're a smart cookie, Lucy. I should be teaching you -'

'But you are!'

Lucy had forgotten about the book in the glovebox until now. She should have insisted on going back to the car. It was too awful to think that Dan-Dad was going to slip back into the shadows at this exact moment in time.

'Is it ever enough?' said Dan-Dad.

'You've taught me how to make tea and breakfast over the past few weeks. I made cheese on toast this morning.'

'I don't think letting an eight-year-old girl become so self-reliant is a good thing.' He paused. 'I didn't even realise you had breakfast this morning.'

Lucy looked around, her chest feeling tight. She could hear her own breath start to whistle.

'Come on, let's go in the water,' she said. 'I know you've got trousers on but you can roll them up and paddle. I'll not go far in,' she promised while clutching Dan-Dad's hand, squeezing hard, desperate to snap him out of his trance.

Dan-Dad merely looked at her, having either heard all or none of it. Lucy stood, swallowing hard to extinguish the volcano in her chest.

'I'm going in the water. I guess you'll watch, then.'

She accepted his nod and strode off towards the water, tip-toeing around the sand worms that littered the wet sand. Lucy gasped as she waded calf-high into the waves, the icy water burning and painting her skin red. She went in further, thigh-deep, waist-deep. She turned to look for Dan-Dad.

He was sitting bolt upright and looking straight ahead, waving his hand vaguely in the direction of the spaniel. It was impossible to tell if he could see her. Lucy was too far out to make out any of Dan-Dad's usual sullen expression. But she could see that his hand had found the dog and had begun to pet it.

Lucy felt the anger bubble up into its own surf at the back of her throat. She could not have her cat, she could not even have a high five or a lousy balloon, but Dan-Dad got his *bloody* dog. It was unfair. None of this was fair. Her Mam was dead and Dan-Dad was even deader, but he got all the sympathy and a dog to fuss over.

Lucy plunged her head down beneath the surface of the water. She almost opened her mouth but managed to hold her breath. She was good at that now. She remembered those first few weeks, when she would creep to the bedroom door and hear Dan-Dad rocking and groaning through his frequent sniffles. She supposed he *had* taught her something: how to hold her breath. Lucy could hold it until Dan-Dad's spasms had stopped. She could even hold it while he was holding his own breath, listening for movement, and time it perfectly so that they both exhaled at the same time. Lucy outlasted him every time as they both sat, their lungs full with hot stale air, listening for each other on the opposite side of the door without ever opening it. This water was a cinch in comparison.

She burst to the surface and stared out at the horizon. Lucy's cheeks felt wetter than the rest of her. Dan-Dad was still sitting like a statue, completely ignoring the dog now. He had not budged an inch, as ever. She went back under and closed her eyes as well as her mouth.

When Lucy rose again, Dan-Dad was halfway between the dunes and the water. He wobbled about on his feet, like he was treading through a minefield.

Lucy dived back under, just as a wave crashed into her back.

Her lips parted.

Her head began to feel light.

Spots began to dance in front of her eyes.

Lucy's mouth ignored the screaming in her head and slowly began to open.

She felt herself being plucked from the sea and gulped in the salted air, her chest heaving and head pounding. The memory of that Christmas night flooded her mind, but her legs were too tired to kick it now.

Dan-Dad did not say a word as Lucy rested on the sand with her head in his lap. He did not say a word as he held up the towel for her to get changed, and nothing on the way back to the car. He stayed silent until she sat in the passenger seat and he turned to her with a face halfway between relief and dread.

'What the hell was that?' he said.

Lucy shrugged and he asked again.

'I was just holding my breath,' she said.

'Nothing else? It was just a game?' Dan-Dad blinked rapidly.

Lucy shook her head.

'Just trying to beat my record.'

Dan-Dad's hand shook and he grabbed the steering wheel.

'I can't do this. We need to go to Auntie Kim's.'

Lucy remembered that the book was still in the glovebox. There was no way Dan-Dad was going to stop off for another burger before they got to Auntie Kim's. She wouldn't have time to put it back into her rucksack. It had to be now.

'Have you seen what's happening over there with the dog?' she said, pointing out of the window. Lucy reached down and began tugging at the zip.

He did not move an inch.

'Stop playing games, Lucy. It's been a damn long day and I don't care about the dog.'

'It's the one from the beach. His owner looks angry with you.'

'What?' he said and turned quickly, arching his neck this way and that.

Lucy opened the glove-box as Dan-Dad turned his head and scooped the book out, aiming for the open bag. It missed and clunked onto the floor with a *thud.*

They both stared at the book.

'What is that?' said Dan-Dad, breaking the silence first.

'It's nothing,' said Lucy, her bottom lip feeling wobbly again. She tried to hide the book behind the bag but Dan-Dad was already starting to lean over into her space.

'Is that a scrapbook?' he asked.

'No, it's nothing.'

'Come on, if it's a scrapbook I want to see it too.' He grabbed the bag to move it and saw the book properly for the first time. His face paled, then spots of red bloomed in his cheeks. 'Is that what I think it is?'

Lucy nodded miserably.

'I'm sorry I took it.'

'Lucy, have you any idea what that book is?'

'It's *A Connecticut Yankee in King Arthur's Court.*'

Dan-Dad shook his head.

'No, it's an early edition of *A Connecticut Yankee in King Arthur's Court.* Do you have any idea how expensive it was? Your mother bought it for me as a birthday present.'

'That's why I took it,' cried Lucy. 'I'm sorry I was a sneak, but Mam always said how much you loved that book. She told me it made you want to be a professor and that it's why you're so clever and say riddles that I don't get. I just wanted to read it too, so that I can be as clever as you and get what you're talking about. I'm sorry.'

The tears that had been pricking at Lucy's eyeballs for the past hour flowed freely now and she squeezed her eyes tightly shut. She felt something pressed into her fist and looked down to see Dan-Dad's handkerchief poking out. Dan-Dad looked out of the window until she had wiped away her final tears.

'Have you read any of it yet?' he asked.

'I only took it last night so I read the first few pages. I put it in my bag and didn't have time to put it back, so I was going to ask you to help me with the bigger words when we got back from Auntie Kim's.'

'You wanted me to teach you about it?'

'Only if you want to.'

Dan-Dad looked out of the window again.

'Your mother told you I liked that book, huh?' his voice, weird and squeaky again.

'She told me it's by your favourite authors. Mark Twain and Suzie's aunt.'

'And who?' Dan-Dad fixed her with a strange expression.

'Mam said you love Twain because his style's like in Suzie's aunt.'

Dan-Dad stared at her. His lips began to twitch and his throat trembled. His eyes creased and he threw back his head and roared with laughter. He shook in his seat and the tears began to flow down his face. As he vibrated and *yuk-yukked* helplessly, Lucy found her own chest and tummy begin to twitch until she was leaning her head against Dan-Dad's shoulder, laughing at his laughter.

Dan-Dad took off his glasses and wiped his eyes.

'The word's insouciant, Lucy, it means -' He lost himself in chuckles again and straightened out in his seat. 'Well, that's something else I'll teach you.' He grinned at her and this time it took longer than usual to slide back into sadness. 'Your mother,' he said. 'I miss her.'

Lucy squeezed his finger.

'I miss her too,' she said.

Dan-Dad smiled his old smile.

'I know,' he said. 'I think I'd just forgotten. Sometimes the ape worries about being selfish so much that it doesn't realise there's more than one form of selfishness.'

Lucy ran her finger down the spine of the book. There were no cracks in it.

'Sorry for taking this,' she said. 'I kept it safe though.'

'You can keep the book,' said Dan-Dad. 'It's like a balloon. You're not supposed to just look at it. You're supposed to make it fart.'

Lucy giggled.

'Shall we read it when we get back from Auntie Kim's?'

Dan-Dad shook his head. 'It's been a long enough day. We can go to Auntie Kim's some other time.'

They drove in silence, one that had no crocodiles lurking under the water. Lucy flicked through the book, squinting when bursts of sunlight crept through the clouds and lit up the pages. She looked up suddenly.

'We didn't have a road-trip in the end,' she said. 'We never even got near the border.'

Dan-Dad kept his eyes on the road. After a moment, he said, 'The most important journeys require no travel.'

Lucy sighed. The quicker she got through this book, the sooner she would understand these puzzles.

Dan-Dad nudged her.

'Here's one you'll get. The greatest gift your mother gave me is not the book. Her best present is present.'

Lucy shrugged.

'We'll get there, Spindleshanks.'

As the car pulled up outside the house, Dan-Dad glanced into the rear view mirror.

'That nosy tomboy from next door looks like she's waiting for you,' he said. 'Why don't you go and tell her about our road-trip while I sort some things out?'

Lucy agreed and skipped across the bright green grass to the fence.

'Hey, Sammy Next-Door. What are you still doing out?'

Sammy rested her chin on the fence.

'I'm just existing with the sunset. You're back early. Bored of the aunt?'

'We didn't go in the end,' said Lucy. 'Went for a burger and played at the beach.'

'Thrilling, I'm sure. How's the zombie?'

'I think he's ok, like real-life ok.'

'He's still weird,' Sammy said, craning her neck to watch Dan-Dad. 'The only dude I've ever known take bin-bags *out* of the car and *into* the house.'

'He's a bit out of it,' said Lucy. 'Probably forgot to do a skip trip with getting up so early. Are you around tomorrow to make a meeting?'

Sammy rolled her eyes.

'*Call*, remember?' She looked thoughtful again. 'Are you around? Not going anywhere with… what's your little name for him?'

Lucy shook her head.

'No plans. I'm not using that nickname anymore. It's a bit babyish.'

'Hmm,' said Sammy. 'Smell you later then.' She got halfway across the garden and stopped. 'I'm glad you're home, you little weirdo,' she said. With that, she disappeared into the house and set about watching the bag removal from the car behind twitching blinds.

Lucy sat on the swing and watched Dan-Dad's long shadow as he began his latest circuit. As the shadow passed, it raised its hand to wave at Sammy in her nest behind the blinds. Lucy reached before her and aligned her own palm with the shadow. High five!

She took the book out of the rucksack and hugged it to her chest. The nickname was definitely too babyish.

From now on, Dad would do just fine.

59

THIS IS NOT A NEXIT

Johnny O

Souhaitez-vous couper votre tête parce-que   merdique? Souhaitez-vous
couper votre tête parce-que   ez-vous couper votre tête
parce-que votre coiffure   r votre tête parce-que votre
coiffure est merdique? S   que votre coiffure est merdique?
Souhaitez-vous couper   e est merdique? Souhaitez-vous
couper votre tête parc   Souhaitez-vous couper votre tête
parce-que votre coiff   couper votre tête parce-que votre
coiffure est merdiqu   rce-que votre coiffure est merdique?
Souhaitez-vous co   fure est merdique? Souhaitez-vous
couper votre tête   e? Souhaitez-vous couper votre tête
parce-que votre   s couper votre tête parce-que votre
coiffure est mer   parce-que votre coiffure est merdique?
Souhaitez-vous   oiffure est merdique? Souhaitez-vous
couper votre   que?   per votre tête
parce-que v   coupe
coiffure
Souhaitez-v   parce-que
couper vo   tre coiffure e   merdique? Souhaitez-vous
parce-qu   merdique? Sou   couper votre tête
coiffure   tez-vous couper
Souha   tête parce-qu   r votre tête
couper   votre coiffure   r votre tête
parce-   merdique? Souh   vous couper   ce-que votre
coiff   itez-vous couper votre tête parce-que   st merdique?
Soul   re tête parce-que votre coiffure   Souhaitez-vous
cou   votre coiffure est merdique? Soul   per votre tête
pa   st merdique? Souhaitez-vous coupé   parce-que votre
co   shaitez-vous coupé votre tête parce-qu   re est merdique?
S   ou   votre coiffure e   ? Souhaitez-vous
                           que   s couper votre tête
                           re est me   ête parce-que votre
          Souhaitez-vo   re est merdique?
          per votre tête par   e? Souhaitez-vous
          parce-que votre coiffu   ous couper votre tête
          coiffure est merdique? So   tête parce-que votre
          dique? Souhaitez-vous couper vo   coiffure est merdique?
          us couper votre tête parce-que votr   ous couper votre tête
          e tête parce-que votre coiffure est merd   tête parce-que votre
          votre coiffure est merdique?. Souhaitez-vou   coiffure est merdique?
          est merdique? Souhaitez-vous couper votre tête p   coiffure est merdique?
          itez-vous couper votre tête parce-que votre coiff   que? Souhaitez-vous
          per votre tête parce-que votre coiffure est merdique   ous couper votre tête
          rce-que votre coiffure est merdique? Souhaitez-vous   arce-que votre
          coiffure est merdique? Souhaitez-vous couper votre tête par   ure est merdique?
          Souhaitez-vous couper votre tête parce-que votre coiffu   merdique? Souhaitez-vous
          couper votre tête parce-que votre coiffure est merdique? Souhaitez-vous couper votre tête

parce-que votre coiffure est merdique? Souhaitez-vous couper votre tête parce-que
coiffure est merdique? Souhaitez-vous couper votre tête parce-que votre coiffure
Souhaitez-vous couper votre tête parce-que votre coiffure est m...
couper votre tête parce-que votre coiffure est merdique?
...est merdique? Souhai...
...haitez-vous couper v...
...votre tête parce-que v...
...e-que votre coiffure est...
...ure est merdique? Souhait...
...? Sou... ...vous couper votr...
...per vo... ...ue votr...
...arce-q... ...t mer...
...oiffure... ...ez-...
...? So... ...têt...

And did those
Walk upon the
And was the
On England's
I AM GRANT

...est merdique?
...Souhaitez-vous
...votre tête
...e votre
...que?

...Souhaitez-vous
...aitez-vous couper votre tête
...re tête parce-que votre
...coiffure est merdique?
...ue? Souhaitez-vous
...couper votre tête
...parce-que votre
...est merdique?
...ouhaitez-vous
...r votre tête
...-que votre
...merdique?
...aitez-vous
...votre tête
...e votre
...dique?
...vous
...ête
...e
...?

Souhaitez-vous couper
couper votre tête parce-q...
...e-que votre coiffure es...
...s est merdique? Souhait...
...us couper votre te...
...arce-que votre...
...fure est merdi...
...uhaitez-vous...
...tête parc...
...e coiffure...
pa...
coiffure...

...re coiffure est...
...rdique? Souhaitez-...
...vous couper votre te...
...te parce-que votre coiffure...
...coiffure est merdique? Sou...
...Souhaitez-vous couper vo...
...e-vous couper votre tête parce-que vo...
...couper votre tête parce-que votre coiffure est merdique?

Souhaitez-vous couper votre tête parce-que votre coiffure est merdique? Souhaitez-vous couper votre tête parce-que votre coiffure est merdique? Souhaitez-vous couper votre tête parce-que votre coiffure est merdique? Souhaitez-vous couper votre tête parce-que votre coiffure est merdique?

Fight, my hand; asant Land

Lards people APOSTROPHE, WILLIAM!

umbers XI.ch

Souhaitez-vous couper votre tête ... re est merdique? Souhaitez-vous
couper votre tête parce-que votre ... Souhaitez-vous couper votre tête
parce-que votre coiffure est merdi ... uper votre tête parce-que votre
coiffure est merdique? Souhaitez-vou ... que votre coiffure est merdique?
Souhaitez-vous couper votre tête p ... est merdique? Souhaitez-vous
couper votre tête parce-que votre coi ... ouhaitez-vous couper votre tête
...e-que votre coiffure est merdique ... per votre tête parce-que votre
...erdique? Souhaitez-vous co ... que votre coiffure est merdique?
...per votre tête parc ... st merdique? Souhaitez-vous
...e votre coif ... aitez-vous couper votre tête
...erdique ... votre tête parce-que votre
...s c ... tre coiffure est merdique?
...dique? Souhaitez-vous
...ous couper votre tête
...tête parce-que votre
...ffure est merdique?
...Souhaitez-vous
...uper votre tête
...e-que votre
...est merdique?
coiffure est merdique? Souhaitez-vous coupe ... Souhaitez-vous
Souhaitez-vous couper votre tête parce-qu ... couper votre tête
couper votre tête parce-que votre coiffure e ... te parce-que votre
parce-que votre coiffure est merdique? Sou ... iffure est merdique?
coif...que? Souhaitez-vous couper v ... que? Souhaitez-vous
s...otre tête parce-que ... couper votre tête
...tre coiffure est ... parce-que votre
...t merdique? Souh ... ffure est merdique?
...aitez-vous couper votre ... dique? Souhaitez-vous
...tête parce-que ... r votre tête
...otre coiffure es ... que votre
...erdique? Souh ... erdique?
...z-vous couper v ... -vous
...ête parce-que ... tête
...tre coiffure est ... tre
...erdique? Souhait ... ?
...vous couper votre
Sou... ...parce-que votre co ... es ... ête
couper v... ...coiffure est merdique Souh...
parce-que vou... ...que? Souhaitez-vous couper ... votre
coiffure est merdi... ...s couper votre tête parce-que ... dique?
Souhaitez-vous co... ...ce-que votre coiffure est ... ez-vous
couper votre tête parc... ...fure est merdique? Souha ... votre tête
parce-que votre coiffure ... ? Souhaitez-vous couper ... -que votre
coiffure est merdique? Sou... ...ouper votre tête parce-que ... est merdique?
Souhaitez-vous couper vou... ...ce-que votre coiffure es ... Souhaitez-vous
couper votre tête parce-que ... ...ure est merdique? Souh ... couper votre tête

PIFFLE PIFFLE PIFFLE

parce-que ... merdique? Souhaitez-vous coup... re
coiffure est ... ous couper votre tête p... ?
Souhaitez-v... parce-que vo... s
couper vot... coiffure ...
parce-que ... lique? S...
coiffure ... vous couper...
Souhait... e parce-que ...
coupe... re coiffure est ...
parc... merdique? Souhai...
coif... ez-vous couper votre ... ?
Sou... te parce-que votre ...
cou... coiffure est merd... ...re tête
pa... ue? Souhaitez-vo... ...ce-que votre
co... ouper votre tête p... e est merdique?
So... que votre coif... Souhaitez-vous
cou... est merdique? ... couper votre tête
pa... ...uhaitez-vous c... tête parce-que votre
coi... ...tre tête parce-... coiffure est merdique?
S... ...r v... re coiffure ... erdique? Souhaitez-vous
c... ...rce-q... lique? Souh...ez-vous couper votre tête
p... ...fure es... ...s cou...er votre tête parce-que votre
c... ...? Souha... ...que votre coiffure est merdique?
c... ...uper votre ... ...est merdique? Souhaitez-vous
... e parce-que v... ...haitez-vous couper votre tête
... re coiffure est n... ...votre tête parce-que votre
... merdique? Souhaitez... ...tre coiffure est merdique?
...uh... vous couper votre tê... ...dique? Souhaitez-vous
couper votre tête parce-que votr... ...z-vous couper votre tête
parce-que votre coiffure est mer... votre tête parce-que votre
coiffure est merdique? Souhait... e votre coiffure est merdique?
Souhaitez-vous couper vo... st merdique? Souhaitez-vous
couper votre tête par... ...ouhaitez-vous couper votre tête
parce-que votre ... couper ...tre ...parce-que votre
coiffure est... e parce-q... ...e est merdique?
S... coiffur... not ceus ...Souhaitez-vous
...diqu... shull my ...per votre tête
...z-vo... we have bu... se-que votre
...otre... Englands gr... merdique?
... itez-vous
c... ...uld to God that a... ...tre tête
pa... ...merdiq... were Prophet ... votre
... ...ez-v... ...lique?
... e tête par... ...vous
c... e votre coiffure est ... tête
... e est merdique? Souhaitez-vous ... ...votre
...? Souhaitez-vous couper votre tête parce-que vou... ...ique?

12

BORIS

Pandora's Box

Jane Carnaffan

The knock on the door in the middle of the night. More like a crash, punctuated by shouting. The old-fashioned 'Police! Open up!', remembered from distant movies. Julia got up slowly. Feeling as though she was moving underwater, she stumbled to the door.

She opened it just before they broke it down.

There were three of them, in their protective suits and masks. They pushed passed her in the narrow hallway. What could she have done?

"You've been reading."

There was silence, as the thoughts ran through her mind. Who could have seen her? Reported her? After all, the Machine couldn't hold control alone, it still needed human agents. But no one came to visit and she had always been so careful, hiding her treasures in the folds of the old sofa. Could it have been one of the drones? She imagined that those little flashing red lights attached to their underbellies, like spiders' eggs, were spy cameras. Perhaps she had a book in her hand as she accepted her daily Calorie delivery. Perhaps she had been getting careless.

"Wouldn't think it to look at her," said another officer. "Butter wouldn't melt."

"Ungrateful bitch!" the third officer half-whispered under his breath.

"You'll have to come with us."

"We'll fix you." The third officer again.

She remembered when they had come for her family. They had barged into their smallholding on the edge of the city. Clumsy hands grabbed the books on environmentalism and organic farming, throwing them to the floor. Heavy boots trampled the allotment, ruining the year's harvest. Staccato voices rapped out a checklist of subversion, lips curled up in disbelief and disgust:

"No Screen, no phone, no internet, no plastic…God! These people!"

They had thought that they'd be safe, where the woods still were, shaded from the scorching sun and far enough away from the suffocating smog.

She hadn't seen her family after that. She learned somehow that they put the real Subversives in Division 1. But how could she know? Maybe she had been imagining a better ending for them, better than working in Division 3 in the factories that created the Calories. Or beyond the Fence where they stripped down outdated electronics to exchange their rare metals for Rations and collected the plastic dumped there to be recycled. Yes, now she remembered, she must have seen it on the Screen. The Machine put out subliminal messages in whispers, in flashing words, in scenes from soap operas. A group of Subversives disguised as Exchange Officers had been caught passing notes inciting revolt to Division 3 workers written on scraps of paper with saved pencil stubs. Like the black spot in Treasure Island. The Machine had generously placed them in Division 1. But why would they put the real Subversives in Division 1? That was what everyone wanted, after all. In Division 1, everyone lived in the new sealed pods, high above the city, where you didn't need to leave your Chair at all. You only needed to think of a coffee drink, or a sugar bar, and it would be there, in liquid form, delivered directly through tubes to your mouth. Or was it veins? Anyway, there was no need to even chew.

She had been assigned to one of the crumbling terraced houses in Division 2. Alone. Unable to leave the house because of the burning sun and toxic smog. She stayed downstairs, sleeping on the lumpy sofa, frightened of the creaking stairs and the scurrying of creatures above. At first she had thought that this was freedom, to be able to slurp on sweet Calorie drinks all day long, to stay up in front of the Screen all night, caffeine buzzing through her veins. As a Division 2 worker, all she had to do was sit in front of the Screen and "like" a few programmes. Not like in Division 1; there they had to work really hard. And then there was no back-breaking work in the allotment and house anymore. No going to bed early and eating healthily, no parents to tell her to fetch this, or do that. But, with a part of her brain that was still free from the Screen, sugar and caffeine, she imagined the scurrying was a mountain stream, passing by an Alpine chalet, surrounded by snow-covered mountains with glaciers tumbling from their slopes. She remembered family holidays in the Alps, but the glaciers had disappeared and the mountains had been swallowed by the Flood long before the Divisions and the Fence.

One day, out of boredom or curiosity, she left the sofa and climbed the stairs, careful to time the expedition between drone deliveries. There were bedrooms with mouldy, unmade beds, dirty clothes tossed on the floor, a forlorn teddy bear with one eye left abandoned. Perhaps the family who lived here had been taken away as her family had been, unexpectedly and brutally. And then she noticed a bookcase in the back room, shelves empty and aching. She reached out to touch where the books had been, almost wishing that one of their ghosts would magically appear in her hands. The bookshelf lurched forward and as she struggled to steady it, she noticed that it had been placed in front of a door. Strange place to put a bookcase! she thought. And forgetting about the next delivery, she tried the door. It opened to narrow stairs, to an attic, filled with the usual detritus of life Before: a derailed rocking horse, staring spookily out of one unseeing painted eye, a rusted scooter, carpet cuttings, a guitar with strings missing, a child's wonky highchair, a pile of wires tangled like tree roots, extinct electronics and boxes, boxes, so many boxes. She half thought she should turn back, remembering she needed to be ready for the next delivery. What would happen if she missed one? Would the drone register and report that she wasn't there, where she should be, in front of the Screen?

But she couldn't resist opening one of the boxes.

As the dust danced in a shaft of golden light - one of the last bursts from a dying sun - she saw that it was filled with books, miraculously dry and unharmed. There were hardbacks, with worn leather covers, their spines embossed in age-tarnished gold: Shakespeare, Dickens, Eliot and Austen. She remembered her brother studying classics like these, writing spidery notes in their margins. Before. In another she found atlases and picture books of "The Stars of the Golden Age of Hollywood" and the "The Impressionists". Another yielded well-

79

thumbed paperbacks, romances, thrillers, crime novels, all chewed around the corners, spines broken with too much love. She stood entranced as though she'd discovered treasures in an ancient tomb.

And then she remembered again. The delivery. She had lost track of time, but surely there must be one soon. It was getting dark outside the little attic window and there was always a delivery at nightfall. She picked up the first book to catch her panicked glance, 'Bleak House', and, with a wry smile at the irony of her choice, fled downstairs. She reached the kitchen window just as the drone was hovering, little red spider eyes flashing.

Her days now passed in the fog-filled, mud-mired streets of Victorian London, submerged in the paper-clogged, soporific demi-monde of the Courts of Chancery. She glided through the brittle, superficial society of Austen's Regency, where the words bounced brilliant, knowing and wry off the dusty pages. She picked up a Mills and Boon, and found she had gobbled up ten in a day, such was the pull of the handsome doctors, mysterious sheiks and alpha-male entrepreneurs. She, like their heroines, just couldn't help herself! The Screen flickered and twitched, she "liked" randomly and occasionally, the drones delivered their Calories and Julia drifted, beguiled by other worlds.

And she remembered the pyre of burning books. They had made a bonfire of the Community's library, inciting her family to throw their treasures into the flames. She realised later that this was a test. Her father, mother and brother had all refused. She, however, had tossed tome after tome into the fire, delighting in the crackle and sparkle as the brittle covers caught light. She was young, rebellious even, bored by her family's dull existence. She later realised that this was why she had been put in Division 2.

These thoughts passed through her head, as she was bundled into the back of the van, blacking out as the third officer forced a cloth filled with noxious fumes over her month. She woke unable to move, her arms and legs restrained, her head foggy and with an ache at the back of her neck. Something warm was trickling down her back. Blood: she could smell its iron scent. A screen in front of her. She struggled, waves of panic running through her. The Screen flickered and flashed up the following message:

"Citizen 1866. Citizen 1866. Do not disconnect. Repeat. Do not disconnect. Concentrate on the 3 Tenets. They will centre you, calm you.

Knowledge is Fragmentary.

Punishment is Reward.

The Maintenance of the Machine is All."

Clamped in the Chair, time passed, messages and tasks constantly flickering before her. Work. So much work. There was always something that required a response. Instantly. Responses to the Machine's ever-expanding drone programme. It seemed even Division 3 workers were earmarked for drone deliveries. Didn't they just slurp Calories from the production line and then sleep on the factory floor? The negative responses only served to highlight the magnanimity of the Machine. She wondered if the comments were real. A sharp shock cascaded through her head and body.

Then there were the responses to the Machine's latest Calorie Campaign. They were generously upping the Calorie intake of Division 1 workers to 5,200 a day, so they could stay awake at their Screens for longer and work more productively. She wondered who was behind the Machine. Was He living in hermetically-sealed luxury with no Screen to serve? Was He free to wander around His apartment, look out onto green gardens, sink His teeth into real food, sip real, fresh water? Would someone draw back the curtain of Control someday and reveal nothing but a mild-mannered man, like in the Wizard of Oz? Or perhaps nothing at all? The pain again. She had been thinking, questioning, imagining.

One day, or maybe night - she no longer knew or cared - she tried to haul herself up from the Chair. She was heavy, her large arms weak, legs swollen and unmoving, a giant ragdoll. Maybe she had forgotten about the new technology, maybe she thought she had to go to the window for a drone delivery, or to the bathroom, but those bodily functions were now serviced in a similar way to Calories. Maybe she was dreaming of going up to the attic, putting her hand into one of the boxes and pulling out a book, like a lucky dip at a summer fair. She didn't know anymore. Thought was now just a response mechanism to the constant demands of the flickering Screen.

She felt a tug at the back of her neck. Messages flashed up on the Screen:

"Citizen 1866, you are disconnected. Citizen 1866, you are disconnected. Reconnect immediately. Repeat. Reconnect immediately."

After what seemed like an age - all her movements, except those of her now uber-nimble fingers, were so slow - she reconnected the USB. Concerned messages flashed up:

"The Machine has registered a malfunction."

"I must have, I don't know, I must have nodded off, I suppose, I don't know."

Her thoughts communicated directly through the wires, electrical pulses tripping through the Machine. The Screen flashed up:

"But it's not Recharge Time yet. We'll send you a Peppy drink. Your usual?"

"Yes, please."

Within seconds a tube was in her mouth, feeding her a sweet, creamy and very strong caffeinated liquid.

"All better, now?"

"All better."

And it was.

Do You Cloop?

K Weismann

'Mind if I sit here?'

Yes.

'Um, no no, not at all.'

'I'm not interrupting you?'

Yes.

'No, no, it's fine.'

'Reading a book?'

Well, I was trying to.

'Mm-hm.'

'Any good?'

No, awful. I often while away hours on end reading terrible books.

'Yeah. Thackeray's *Book of Snobs.*'

'What's it about?'

The expansion and subsequent collapse of the South Sea Bubble.

'Um, snobs.'

'Ah, right. Well, carry on.'

I flickered an appreciative smile as he resumed supping his pint, in the assured knowledge that I would not for long be permitted to carry on with my book. There is something about sitting in a pub with a book that seems to send out waves of radiation alerting lone drinkers - who don't have a book for company, who wouldn't consider a book company at all - that here is a lonely soul in need of cheery conversation to pep them up in their solitude. That man is all alone, they say. All alone in the world. See, he has to resort to reading a book in the pub, poor friendless creature that he is. Someone to talk to is what he needs. And I in my infinite charity am the man (for it almost exclusively will be a man) to step up to the job. Now I am sure these fellows are well-intentioned, as knights-errant of yore were in their divinely-inspired personal crusades. But I am not lonely. I am alone, true. But I have a book. I am happy with my book. But it is difficult to read that book with you skirmishing 'round the walls with your aries and corax and your ballista bombarding me with boulders of small talk. Not very hospitable of you, you might say. Well, perhaps not. Perhaps I'm not very hospitable. But I just want to read my book. Is that so strange? I just want to be left alone. But no, see now, here he is again, as predicted.

'So what's it say?'

'Well, it's just a kind of witty commentary on various types of snob in Victorian England.'

He scowled. What possible use could there be in reading such a book? his crumpled face seemed to say. It's a complete waste of time. I must get to the root of this delusion and rip it out and free him from his agony.

'Learnt anything?' It was politer at least than my physiognomical interpretation.

'Well... nothing *practical*, I guess. It's not a Haynes manual.'

Actually, it kind of is. But I wasn't about to try to explain that.
'I learnt I can cloop.'
'Eh?'
'I learnt I can cloop. And pour.'
'You can cloop?'
'Thackeray describes the sound of a cork being forcibly drawn from a bottle as a cloop. Quite neat, don't you think?'

'And you can cloop?' His brow was knitted now in solicitous furrows. This man, he thought, is a lunatic. He's gone peculiar in his isolation.

'And pour. It's the only decent impression I can do, really. Listen.' And I demonstrated my impression of a cork being pulled from a bottle and its contents poured into a glass. And a fine impression it was, I thought.

'Hm.' He was unmoved.

'Well, it amuses me anyway...'

'Aye, it's not bad. More of a toc though, I'd say, than a cloop. Sounds more like the cork in a whisky bottle than a wine bottle.'

The maven of clooping suddenly!

'Anyway, that's not really a take-home lesson of the book. Just an aside.'

'Hm.' And he returned to his pint.

I continued reading my Thackeray. Ostensibly, at least. For in actuality I was gazing blankly at the pages, turning over and over in my head my attempt at clooping. Silently, from memory, of course - I could hardly sit there clooping away like a madman struck out of the blue with some species of Tourette's or palilalia! To tell the truth I had always been rather proud of my uncork-and-pour impression, as I had heretofore referred to it. It had put smiles on many a face at parties in my younger days, and could still be relied on for some little amusement even now. But no sooner do I put a name to my small feat than I am shot down at no less than its debut showing! And presently, as I inwardly gnashed and growled and mumbled and grumbled, another chap showed up at our table.

'Hallo, Bob!' exclaimed my soi-disant new friend in tones of long familiarity. 'How's you? Pull up a pew, man!' - at which he turned with frankly too overt deference to myself - 'That's alright, isn't it, you don't mind?'

Mumble grumble...

'No no, of course...'

'Sure you don't mind?' The obsequious Bob.

Do I have an option? Mr Bob Sequious? Hah!

'Not at all, no...'

And they fell into conversation of thises and thats, heres and theres, hims and hers and raucous nothings; and I fell back to my blind book-staring, when my companion - the original one, let us call him Porlock - came out with:

'This fella can cloop, y'know.'
'Cloop?'
'And pour,' I added, though Heaven alone knows why. 'Aye, and pour.'
'And pour?'
'Aye,' - and to myself - 'eh?'
'Mm-hm.'
'Cloop and pour, eh?'

'Aye.'

'Mm-hm.'

'Whassat then?'

'It's in Thackerley -'

'- Thackeray -'

'- Thackeray. It's the force of a... No, hang on...'

'The sound of a cork being forcibly drawn from a bottle.'

'That's a cloop?'

'That's a cloop.'

'And the pour?'

'That's a pour.' A dead pause. 'Of wine. I added that myself.'

'Oh aye?'

I felt it incumbent upon me to elucidate. A second performance. My mouth was dry. I took a sip of my ale and swallowed narrowly.

A passing fair cloop, I adjudged.

If Porlock had been unmoved, Bob was as an Easter Island head; grimly stony, greyly unblinking. Eyes hooded and sightless.

'Uhrrr...' - it was both a moue and a moo - 'More of a ploc than a cloop, I'd say...'

'I thought a toc.'

'The pour was alright, though.'

Oh, jolly dee!

'More like a bottle of rum, though.'

'I said whisky.'

'Aye. A shorter, shallower ploc -'

'- toc, than a -'

'- than a cloop.'

'But the pour was good.'

'Aye, the pour was good. The pour was like wine.'

'Aye, the pour was like wine. Too long for whisky.'

'Or rum.'

'Or rum. But it was good wine.'

'If it was the second glass from a bottle of wine -'

'Aye.'

'- with the cork just pushed back in, so it's not a long...'

'Cloop.'

'- cloop.'

'More of a toc.'

'Or ploc. Aye, that'd work.'

I fumed. I boiled and simmered.

'*Ploc, toc!* OK, you cloop.'

Porlock havered. He couldn't, he said. Loose larynx. Bob stepped up.

'What was that? That wasn't a cloop. That was more of a... more of a *platch.*'

'A platch?'

'You know, a kind of splashing, slopping sound. Like a wet leaf falling.' Definitely a lunatic. 'Or a man trudging through mud.'

'Never heard of platch.'

'You'd never heard of cloop!'

'Aye, but that's in Thackerley.'

'Thackeray! And you'd never heard of him either!'

'Aye, but he's a writer.'

'I'm a writer!'

'But I've never heard of you.'

'You'd never heard of Thackeray!'

'Aye, but he's got a book.'

'I've got a book!'

'Where's your book?'

'Well, I don't carry copies of it around with me!'

'I'll Google it. What's it called? Platch?'

'No! It's nothing to do with platching! And I didn't make up platch!'

'Well, who made up platch? Was that Thackerley too?'

'*Thackeray* didn't just spend his career making up onomatopoeic words!'

'Shakespeare?'

'Dickens?'

'I've no idea! I think it's a Scots word.'

'The Scots made it up, then?'

'You can't just go around making up words.'

'Well, ultimately all fucking words are made-up, aren't they, you -!'

The apposite phrase tripped and fell on its way out. Mercifully. A cowed silence fell.

I stared blankly at my book. This is why *my* middle name isn't Makepeace. I tried to regain some composure.

'So then the word for your impression would be ploc?'

'Or toc.'

'It's a cloop...' - feebly, like the last few drops of grey bathwater being wrung out of a wet flannel.

'I dunno like...'

'Oh, look!' Bob suddenly exclaimed, noticing an acquaintance across the bar - presumably a *doctor litterarum* learned in all the words of the world who might clear the whole farrago up once and for all - and proceeded to bellow: 'Heya! Estelle! Heya!'

Estelle presented herself. She was what might well be described as a bonny lass. Bonny, in that oft-used (if the yardstick of my experience is in concord with the mode) sense of the word: attractive, yes, but could advisably do with sloughing off a good few handfuls of avoirdupois, shall we say.

'Hallo, Bob.'

Everyone knew Bob, it would seem. I wished I knew Bob, so that I could without being thought ill-humoured tell him to -

'This fella can cloop.'

'Cloop?'

'And platch.'

'I can't platch!'

'Sorry,' Porlock corrected himself: 'and pour.'

'What's a cloop?'

'It's the sound of a force...' he began. 'No, hang on...'

'It's the sound of a cork being forcibly drawn from a bottle,' I reiterated.

'And you're a clooper?'

'Well, he's a writer, so he says.'

'But he hasn't got a book.'

'Well, he has, so he says.'

'But you can cloop?'

And I had scarcely even parted my lips to utter an explanation of any of this, when again Porlock interjected with his:

'Well, so he says! But we reckon -'

And here Bob intrajected:

'Whoa! Don't tell her! See what she makes of it.'

All eyes and ears were on me. The difficult third act.

I clooped.

I poured.

Exactly the same as the other renditions.

Bob and Porlock turned to Estelle, like the Israelites at the foot of Mount Sinai.

'Hm. I'd say it was more of a sloop.'

'A sloop!?'

'This is a cloop.'

She cleared her throat, and clooped. Badly, I would hasten to add.

'That was a clock.'

'Well, at least it wasn't a sloop.'

'A sloop, honestly!'

'A sloop? A sloop's like a...' Porlock was lost again. 'Like a...?'

'A sailing vessel,' I explained wearily.

'Like Sloop John B?'

'Like Sloop John B.'

'But it's not a sloop,' said Bob. 'I mean, not a sloop like a sloop, like Sloop John B. A sloop like a *sloop*. It's not a long sound.'

'Oh no,' Estelle agreed, 'it's like a whisky bottle.'

'See, I said whisky.'

'Or it could be rum.'

'Or it could be rum.'

'But not wine.'

'No, not wine.'

'It's too short.'

'Yeah, it's too short for wine. Unless it were the second glass.'

'Unless it were the second glass, aye, I said that.'

'So I guess,' Estelle concluded, 'more of a slop, then.'

'A slop!?' I was affronted. 'It's a cloop, damn it!'

'The pour was good, though,' she added. Comfortingly, I think was the intent.

'Aye, the pour was good.'

'True. The pour was good.'

'That was like wine.'

'It was like wine.'

'But the cloop -'

'- it was more of a ploc -'

'- or a toc -'

They continued. On an on. And on and on. 'Round and 'round and 'round and 'round. Ceaselessly, like an ouroboros. They may still be there, I do not know. Me, I made my excuses amongst fitful bursts of Sloop John B and betook myself, my ale, and my Thackeray to the other side of the pub, to an empty table in the corner far away from such goings on.

*****

'And it seems to me that all English society is cursed by this mammoniacal superstition; and that we are sneaking and bowing and cringing on the one hand, or bullying and scorning on the other, from the lowest to -'

'Excuse me?'
'Hm?'
'Mind if I sit here?'
'Hmmm. It depends.'
'I'm sorry?'
'Do you cloop?'

The Boar

Aurora Cording

Ah Christ, it's Kev! An' 'e's clocked me. Ah well, no avoidin' 'im, ah guess. 'Ere goes.

- A'reyt.
- A'reyt.
- Wai'in' fer ' 225?
- Nah, ' 254.
- A'reyt.

- 'Ah's *errr...* Janice?
- Aye, a'reyt.
- Ah, reyt.
- 'Ah's ye?
- Aye, reyt.
- Ah, reyt.

- Bin up t' much?
- Nah, n' much.
- Ah, reyt.
- Ye?
- Nah, n' really.
- Aye, reyt.

- 'Sat like?
- Book ah'm readin'.
- Ah, reyt.
- Aye.
- 'Sany good?
- Aye.
- 'Sit like?
- Ahh, 'sa bunch o' short stories. 'Sun's brilliant like.
- A'reyt.
- 'Sabaht a bloke gets stuck up a tree wi' a boar.
- A'reyt.
- Aye. 'Sbrilliant.
- Aye?
- 'Slike... 'Slike me'aphysical like.

- A'reyt.
- Aye.
- So... Wh'appens?
- Well, nowt. 'E's jus' stuck up a tree.
- Wi' a boar? Like a pig?
- Aye.
- Stuck in a tree wi' a pig?
- Aye, well -
- 'Ah'd a pig ge' in a tree?
- Well, 'e's not *wi'* the pig in the tree.
- ...
- The pig's at ' bottom o' ' tree. The pig *chased* 'im up ' tree. An' it's a boar.
- A'reyt.
- ...
- So the pig chased 'im up a tree?
- Boar.
- Boar, reyt.
- Aye.
- Then wh'appens?
- Well, nowt, 'e's jus' stuck up a tree.
- Ah, reyt.
- 'Sme'aphysical like.
- A'reyt.
- Like *ahh*... Like Wai'in' fer Godot.
- Were that wi' Stephanie Beacham?
- Nah, that were Stephanie Cole.
- From Tenko?
- No, that were Stephanie Beacham.
- Stephanie Cole were in Tenko, weren't she?
- No, that were... Actually, they were both in Tenko. But ah'm talkin' abaht Wai'in' fer God.
- Ah don't remember a pig in Wai'in' fer God.
- *Ah!* Ah mean Wai'in' fer Godot, not Wai'in' fer God!
- Ah, reyt. 'Sat go' a pig in it, then?
- No.
- A'reyt.

- Ah mean it's me'aphysical like Wai'in' fer Godot.
- A'reyt. S'wh'appens, then?
- In Wai'in' fer Godot?
- Aye.
- Nowt.
- A'reyt.
- Tha's the point.
- A'reyt.
- 'Sjus' me'aphysical discourse.
- A'reyt.
- They're jus'... *wai'in' fer Godot.*
- A'reyt. No pig, then?
- No. That's jus' this story. An' it's a boar.
- A'reyt.
- See?
- Aye. So 'e's up a tree wi' a pig at ' bottom, and nowt 'appens.
- No, 'e reflects, 'e ponders, 'ow 'e's up a tree wi' a pig at ' bottom.
- Well, 'e mus' know!
- Aye, 'e *knows!* Course 'e *knows.* But 'e's *pond'rin'* 'ow ridiculous it is, 'e's *pond'rin'* the absurdity o' the situation. 'Sa me'aphor fer the 'uman condition.
- Ah, reyt.
- See?
- Nah.
- 'E's in the foot'ills o' ' Pyrenees, an' 'e comes across a pig -
- 'Sit a pig or a boar?
- *Argh!* It's -
- 'Ang on, is this your story or Wai'in' fer Goddo?
- Neither of 'em are *my* story. Wai'in' fer Godot were by Samuel Beckett -
- Ah! From Quan'm Leap?
- What?
- Wi' a pig? Ah remember, is this the Buddy 'Olly episode?
- What? No!
- Ah don' remember Buddy 'Olly ge'in' stuck up a tree like...
- This is nowt to do wi' Quan'um Leap.
- Ah, reyt. So...

- It's nowt to do wi' it.
- A'reyt.
- And it's not *my* story.
- A'reyt.
- 'Sa comple'ely independen' story.
- 'Baht a man up a tree.
- Yeh. Well -
- Why's 'e up a tree?
- Well, it's symbolic, i'nit? Like in The Seventh Seal.
- Eh?
- The Seventh Seal. Ingmar Bergman.
- 'Er from Casablanca?
- *Ingmar* Bergman.
- Nah.
- Ohh, where's me bus?

- S'wh's'appenin' nah, then? Still pond'rin'?
- 'E c'n see smoke on ' 'orizon.
- Ah, reyt. 'Sat then?
- Prob'ly forest fires.
- Nah, ah mean... 'Sat symbolize?
- Ah, ah dunno.
- 'Ah'd'y'know it's symbolic if y'don' know wha' it symbolizes?
- Well, ah don' know *yet.*
- Ah, reyt.
- ...
- So when d'y'find out? 'S'ere like a a twist at ' end? Like a big reveal?
- Nah, 'snot really that kind o' story.
- So then, 'ah'd'y'know?
- Well, y'jus' kinda work i' out.
- Eh?
- Y'jus'... 'ave t' figure i' out fer yerself.
- Y'jus' figure i' out fer yerself?
- Yeh, basic'ly.
- Nob'dy tells y'?
- Well, nah.
- 'Sno' wri'en in there?

- Well, no' in so many words.
- Eh?
- No' direc'ly, nah.
- So then...
- ...
- 'Ow?
- Well, y'read it. An' figure i' out. Reread it, if needs be.
- Sahnds a lo' of effort.
- N' really. Y'd watch a film more'n once, if i' were complica'ed.
- Nah.
- Ah, reyt.
- Ah dunno if ah c'd do tha'.
- Mebbe not.
- Ah dunno 'ah ye can.
- Ah dunno righ' nah.
- Ah dunno. *Phe-ewww!*

- Fires still goin'?
- In ' distance.
- 'Sa'reyt then.
- Well, 'e'll 'ave t' replan 'is route.
- Ah though' 'e were stuck up a tree.
- 'E is righ' nah.
- So dun' really mek any diff'rence then.
- Well, 'e migh' be cu' off. 'E migh' no' be ebble t' ge' through t' where 'e's goin'. No' by ' route 'e were gonna tek.
- Ah'd be more worried abaht ' boar.
- Well, righ' nah, aye. Bu' at some poin' -
- 'Ah'd 'e ge' chased up a tree by a boar anyway?
- Well, 'e were walkin', an' 'e stumbled across ' piglets. 'N' then ' boar cem chargin' aht o' ' undergrowth.
- 'N' 'e climbed a tree?
- Aye, well -
- Well, nah 'e's stuck! 'S'is own faul'! 'E shou'n'ta climbed ' tree!
- Bu' i' were a choice o' climbin' a tree or ge'in' gored by a boar.
- Ah'da fough' ' boar.
- Would y' nah?

101

- Aye. Ah c'd figh' a boar. 'Sjus' a pig.
- A boar'd do some damage like.
- Ah reckon ah'd be reyt.
- A'reyt.
- Ah'd no' be stuck up a tree!
- Nah, y'd be mangled at ' bottom of a tree.
- Y'd climb ' tree like?
- Well, aye, y'd 'ave t', ah reckon.
- Nah. Nah, no' me. Ah'd be reyt.
- Ah, reyt.

- 'Cordin' t' this there's no 254s runnin'.
- Eh?
- Checked on ' buses while y' 'ad yer nose in yer book. Bin an accident.
No 254s runnin'. 225 should be 'ere in 'baht twenny minutes though.
- ' 225 teks ages.
- Nice bus journey. Teks abaht an hour t' my 'ouse.
- Abaht ' sem to mine. Hmmm.
- Ah well. No rush.
- Y're callin' a taxi? Bi' extravagan', i'nit?
- Ah really need t' ge' back.
- Ah, up t' ye, ah guess. Ah'm wai'in fer ' bus.
- Aye, nah, that'll tek too long fer me. Taxi should be 'ere in a couple
o' minutes.
- Ah, reyt. Well, see y' 'rahnd.
- A'reyt.
- A'reyt.

Thank God fer that! Don' think ah coulda coped wi' much more o' that.
'Ome.' Ome 'n' a cuppa's wha' ah need.
There 'e goes, wavin' away. There 'e -
Wait, wha's 'e up t'?
Ohhh, wha' nah?

- 225s're all cancelled 'n' all. Any chance ah c'n share yer taxi, since
we're goin' ' sameish way?
- Uh, yeh... Course.

- Cheers, mate.
- No problem.
- Ah, 'sbe'er. Nice 'n' warm 'n' comfy. This is more like i'.
- Mm.
- So - wha'ever 'appened to ' fella up ' tree. 'E ge' away from ' boar?

Grandad's Garden

Peter Jones

The apples were rotting on the ground in the orchard and the grass was overgrown. Rust-tinged petals had fallen from late roses and the gate was hanging from a creaking hinge. Everywhere I looked there was evidence of neglect in my grandfather's garden. The multi-greyed skies seemed low enough to touch. A sudden gust chilled my bones.

I sighed deeply as I turned toward the house, its back door looking sorrowful with flaking green paint and what appeared to be a crack in one of the wood panels. The glass panels and the rear windows were covered in grime and I noticed that the guttering was hanging down at one end.

Higher up, a single crow shared the chimney pot with a sapling.

I fumbled in my overcoat pocket to find the bunch of keys that the solicitor had given me two days previously. He'd found me on LinkedIn and called me at my Vancouver office a little over a week ago. I'd picked up my hire car at Manchester Airport and, with the help of satnav, drove straight to his small office in Burnley.

'Ah, Mr Peters.' He held out a thin, bony hand. His grip was surprisingly firm. He stood a good two inches taller than me and it made him look almost brittle.

'Yes. Mr Richardson?'

We settled in his office, each side of a large but modern desk.

'When did you last see your grandfather?'

'I was a child. Eight? Maybe nine years old. About half a century ago. We emigrated to Canada in 1965. At first I wrote about once a month. But, as I grew older, the writing tailed off and I was overtaken by life itself. You know, college, marriage, family, business. Grandad faded. Four-and-a-half thousand miles is a lot now, but it was even more so then.'

'Quite so, Mr Peters. Anyway, down to business. I understand that both of your parents are dead and that your mother was an only child, as you are?'

'Yes.'

'Your grandfather, Thomas Philbert, spent the last eight or nine years in a home, paid for by a substantial sum he'd accumulated over his lifetime. However, his house lay empty throughout all that time.' He opened a drawer and took out a bunch of keys. Passing them over to me, he said: 'The house and all its contents have been left to you, along with a sum of ...' - he hesitated as he looked down at the papers on his desk - 'ah yes, £108,963 - after all disbursements. You just need to sign the documents. But please read them first.'

'Thanks. There's no need. I read the PDF files you emailed me.'

I signed and took the keys, along with Grandad's death certificate, and drove to the Premier Inn on the edge of the town centre.

I spent the next day wandering about the town. The football ground was still there, though it's looking better than I remembered. Walking under the canal aqueduct toward the centre of town, now pedestrianised, I wondered what I'd remember. It had all changed. I don't know why it surprised me. The old municipal college is now a madrasah, so the receptionist in the hotel had told me earlier. 'There's a new college opposite ASDA now,' she'd said. ASDA? I didn't know where that was anyway. By early evening I'd had enough of trying to recall my boyhood playgrounds in the town centre and the terraced streets of the 1960s. I found what looked like a decent curry house. I wasn't disappointed. An hour and a bit later I walked past the old college and read the signs at the entrance. I assumed the other languages were Urdu and Arabic. After a pint and a whisky chaser in the Queen Victoria next to the hotel, I decided to call it a day. In the hotel room I watched the News at Ten until I drifted off.

I awoke to the sound of BBC News 24, but didn't pay much attention. I left it on whilst I showered and dressed. Then suddenly my attention was drawn to the news. There'd been a terrorist attack in Paris. I let out a sigh of despair as I thought about the waste of life, the destruction of friendships and the mindless would-be revenge attacks on innocent people. As a child I had many friends from both Catholic and Muslim families. Back home in Vancouver, the firm's multicultural policy was highly successful and I wondered about the safety of my colleagues there, too.

In the pub I breakfasted on scrambled eggs and The Guardian, trying to make sense from the senseless killings. But I also had Grandad on my mind. Putting the paper aside I took out the keys I'd been given, weighing them in my palm, I decided it was time to go. I pulled in at the large Tesco and bought a sandwich, a bottle of carbonated water and a small flashlight.

*

I looked at the bunch and chose what looked like a back door key. I tested the keyhole, and, with a bit of pressure, it unlocked. As I suspected, the electric was off so I took the flashlight from my pocket. After a small struggle, I managed to raise the blinds on the kitchen window. What light came through showed a film of dust on everything. Memories slowly filtered through my mind - I could almost smell my Granny's home-baked biscuits. I made my way to the door which opened into the hallway. Despite the dust, I could see the Victorian tiles that stretched from the kitchen door to the wide front door and into the porch beyond. Entering the dining room, I pulled aside the curtains and looked out at the garden. The dirt made everything look even grimmer than it did just a few moments earlier. I turned back and saw the old furniture - table, six chairs, a sideboard - and wondered if the crockery and cutlery were still in the drawer. But I didn't bother looking.

In turn I entered two rooms at the front of the house. The living room, where my grandparents spent most of the time, and the parlour - only used on special occasions, or when the parish priest came round. It doubled up as a home library. Both of my grandparents were avid readers and one wall was covered with shelves of books, dictionaries, philosophy, poetry, novels and guide books. They travelled a lot.

Both rooms were in much the same state as all the other rooms.

I decided not to bother with the cellar, reached by the cupboard under the stairs, but something was nagging at the back of my mind.

Upstairs, the two large bedrooms, the two smaller ones and the bathroom didn't give up any surprises.

I took out my cell phone and looked for the solicitor's number. I asked him about the utility providers. He said he'd sort it for me. He told me he'd arrange for a surveyor to come round too. Thanking him, I called my wife.

'Keith! What's the …? What is it? It's almost 3:30. Is everything alright?'

'Sorry, Anna. I forgot the time difference. It's what ...?' - I checked my watch - 'eight hours? I'll call you about midday, your time. Nothing serious, speak later, go back to sleep.'

'I'll try, honey. Good night. I mean morning. Speak later.'

I decided to look in the attic. The door was a bit stiff and the stairs creaked. The roof light needed a clean but there was enough light for me to see. A few books were scattered around along with the odd old newspaper. Sitting on an old chest, I decided to stay a while longer in East Lancashire and see what I could do with the place.

I returned to the hotel and turned on the iPad. It immediately searched out the Wi-Fi and prompted me to put in the password. After a few moments I found it in the hotel information folder. I typed it in and, presto, I was connected to the whole world. I looked for local tradesmen and made a note - plumbers, electricians, builders, cleaners. I hadn't realised at the airport, but I noticed that British postal codes are similar to those in Canada.

I made some notes using the pad and the cheap pen provided by the hotel.

I went down to reception and asked for a local street map and the receptionist passed me one from under the counter. It was little more than a sketch with scant detail.

'You been to Burnley before?'

'Yes, but not for many years.'

'You American?'

'Canadian.' Showing her my notes, I asked if she knew of any tradesmen.

'Billy Builder's my cousin,' she said, in that broad East Lancashire accent that, despite the years, I found both familiar and comforting. 'Bill does most jobs around the 'ouse, an' he knows a 'lectrician an' a plumber. You thinking of buying an 'ouse round 'ere?'

'Something like that.'

I went back to my room and gave Billy a call. He said he knew where it was and we arranged to meet the following day.

I called Mr Richardson and updated him. He said he'd try to get the utility reps there tomorrow as well. I told him I'd be there at about eleven.

After lunch - we called it dinner when I was a lad - I decided to see more of the town. I followed my nose, as my Gran would have said all those years ago, and found new roads and buildings had popped up everywhere but many of the old familiar ones still stood testament to their Victorian heritage. On the edge of town the old boys' grammar school now seemed to be part of the University of Central Lancashire, wherever that is. I continued into the centre, found a bench and sat for a while, trying to get my bearings. A wrought iron signpost pointed to way to Tourist Information. I found it in the old Mechanics' Institute, now a theatre and art gallery, looking much better than it did when I was a kid. Five minutes later I was armed with a handful of leaflets, a guide book and a more detailed street map. Continuing my exploration, I found a coffee shop and ordered an Americano. Over here too? When did it get so difficult to order a simple mug of black coffee? Choosing a window seat, I settled down to some reading.

My mind kept drifting back to my Grandad's house and how sorry it all looked. I decided to do more wandering before returning to my room. By early evening I was getting peckish. 'Yeah, there's the Queen Vic 'ere,' the receptionist responded to my enquiry.

'Something not quite so pubbish?'

'Oh yeah, plenty in town,' - pointing it out on the map I showed her - 'This is a great one.'

'Thanks.'

Twenty minutes later I was shown to a table with perhaps a dozen other early diners for company. After-dinner coffee was surprisingly good and looking at my watch, I decided to call Anna.

'Hi, honey. What's it like?'

'Grey', I said. We chatted about kids and grandchildren, the dog, the business and the Paris shootings. 'Anna, I think I need to stay awhile.'

'What? How long? What about the business?'

'I don't know. The house needs a bit of care. It needs to be sale-ready and I don't know how long that'll take. I've got people coming in the morning, I'll know more then. It'll be more than the week we'd planned. But I'll still be home by Christmas. I'll call Farzana in an hour or so and let her know. She's run the show before.'

'Before Christmas? Keith, we're only halfway through November! How long's it going to take?'

'I don't know, Anna. I'll call you again tomorrow after I've spoken to everyone. OK?'

'OK, I understand. I just thought you'd be home next week. Use your iPad and we can Skype. I'll get the grandkids round. Bye, honey, speak tomorrow.'

'Good night, Anna. Speak - well, see you tomorrow.'

I hung up and watched the good old BBC. But it was all about the Paris attack.

*

The next day I arrived at the house and found a man leaning against his van, an old VW, and having a smoke.

'Billy?'

'Yeah. Mr Peters, is it?'

'Call me Keith. We'll try the front door. I've not used it yet. I noticed a pile of mail yesterday. I'll sort that while you look around. There's no electricity though. You got a flashlight?' I looked up at the ever-grey skies, but it didn't look like rain. 'You can pull your van onto the drive if you like.' There was plenty of room for two vehicles. As he did so, I opened the door. It was stiff and the hinges gave out a small high-pitched groan. But it was in surprisingly good condition. Underneath the dirt of years, it was the same colour green as those park benches from my childhood. The opening of the door swept an arc through the piles of letters, leaflets and free newspapers. I picked them up and placed them on a small table in the porch and stepped inside the hallway. A moment or two later Billy joined me.

'When's the 'leccy man coming?'

'This morning, I hope. Do you want to start at the top and make your way down to the ground floor? I think the cellar's out of the question until we've got light.' The November light was just about good enough to see by and he clambered up the stairs, pencil behind his ear and toolbox in hand.

I decided to sift the mail - junk and maybe not junk. After a few minutes the junk pile was about three times the size of the other pile. I wondered what they did about recycling. I started on the smaller pile. Another two piles. To deal with and too late to deal with. About halfway through I found a letter from my Great Aunt Jessica, my Gran's sister. I could just about remember her. I looked at the date. 2008. Seven years ago, just after my grandad had gone into the home. She was asking about Gran, said she hadn't seen or heard from her in a while and was very worried because my Grandad hadn't replied to her recent letters. I wondered if Aunty Jessica was still alive. Her phone number must be around somewhere. I put the letter in my coat pocket. The rest of the mail seemed to be utility bills. They'd be sorted when the reps turned up.

Throughout the day people came and went, utilities were checked, declared safe and switched on. However, the electric company rep thought that the house hadn't been rewired since the 1960s. The surveyor arrived and he and Billy spent quite a time inside and outside the house, climbing ladders, looking at the roof, testing for damp and woodworm. They agreed that and work was minor and cosmetic. Even the cellar got a clean bill of health. I talked to Billy and arranged for a complete rewire, a new kitchen and new bathroom. He gave me the online contact for the council, said ta-ra and he'd be back in the morning.

I thought I'd take a quick look in the cellar before returning to the hotel. The stairs creaked slightly and the handrail needed tightening. The single unshaded light was good enough to see by, but wasn't great. I could see the echoes of life all over the cellar - an old kitchen table, a wooden trunk, a couple of old suitcases, a toolbox, a workbench, an old broken umbrella, a tea chest, boxes and lots and lots of just the stuff of life. I decided to have a closer look the next day.

As I turned to go back up, I noticed an old wooden filing cabinet under the stairs. It was locked and I assumed the key was with the bunch I'd left on the table in the porch.

Well, it'd have to wait till tomorrow morning.

*

Being used to hotels on expenses, I'd forgotten how soulless places like the Premier Inn could be. Okay for a couple of nights, perhaps three or four, but I was going to be here for at least a month. I decided to look up estate agents; perhaps I could get a short-term furnished apartment. The hotel's notepad was to come in handy. I jotted down a few names and checked the addresses against the street map. As I pored over it, I tried to visualise my childhood world - the park, the football ground with the cricket club next to it, the Sparrowhawk Hotel, the old boys' grammar school, the Town Hall - quite a few familiar buildings, but the change was incredible.

I needed a drink, but didn't fancy the pub next door. I drove to the Sainsbury's I'd noticed by the old grammar school and picked up a bottle of Lagavulin, a good peaty Scotch, and returned to the hotel for an evening of British TV.

After about twenty or so minutes my iPad chirruped. It was Anna, Skyping. Morgan and Freya, our granddaughters, sat with their Gran, beaming smiles across the Atlantic. No pen and ink for them, instant communication at the speed of light. A change for the better, in my view, though I could still mourn the lost art of letter writing.

Forty-plus minutes of chat and family stuff and the girls were so eager to tell me all about the rehearsals for the school Christmas play, oh, and Jasper, the new puppy had chewed Dad's slippers and Mom was starting her new job in the new year, Assistant Librarian at the university.

'Is it night there, Grandad?'

'Yes, Morgan, it's after nine here.'

Though it was out of my sight, I could see the kids looking at the kitchen clock. 'You better go to bed,' said Freya.

'Too darn right. Good night, girls.'

'Good afternoon, Grandad.' Almost in unison.

'I better go, Anna. Much to do tomorrow. I'll call or text. Bye, honey.'

'Bye. Love you.'

The screen went blank and so did my mind.

*

Petty's estate agents showed me a small, unfurnished terraced house on Shorey Bank, right next to the madrasah. The agent said I could have it on a three month rental and it came with a single parking space. Without much thought, I signed the documents and paid upfront. I spent the rest of the day buying stuff from charity shops and filling the house. However, the combination microwave was new, as were the bed and mattress, and, TV. And I'd need to sort out internet access.

The next day I went to Grandad's house to catch up on everything. As I stood in the back garden I took in my surroundings. It was a grey Lancashire morning. It's funny how my memories of childhood were full of colour and I'd almost forgotten how low the sky seemed here.

I was determined to explore the filing cabinet in the cellar and wondered what I'd discover. Old photos, perhaps, or official documents, the odd love letter, maybe a war medal or two; even Aunt Agatha's phone number. I was looking forward to it.

None of the keys fitted so I looked around the cellar for something to lever open the drawers. I found a large flat-blade screwdriver with a broken red handle and that did the trick.

Each drawer was full of papers and cards of all sorts - birthdays, anniversaries, Christmas, a box of postcards from seaside resorts. One drawer held a bundle of letters and I recognised them at once. They were from me. I'd be here all day if I started to read them, so I placed them on the steps and continued foraging. The bottom drawer contained a box full of photographs and negatives. Memories frozen in time, in sepia, in black and white, in colour. Recorded life, curled and faded but viewable, nevertheless. This was another job to put off. Taking out the box, I found some more letters, carefully placed to lie as flat as possible on the bottom of the drawer, as if they'd been hidden. They all seemed to have the same handwriting.

I remembered my Great Aunt Jessica's letter and took it from my coat pocket. The writing was the same. As I bundled them up, I wondered why my Grandad, or someone else, had wanted to hide them. If they didn't want anyone to see them, why not just burn them? I placed these on the steps too.

A box file yielded birth and marriage certificates, wartime ID's, and an old blue passport. The filing cabinet held the records of life, a family archive. I decided that the lot would be shipped to Canada so that I could study it all in more detail. I put my letters back but, for some reason, I thought I'd take Great Aunt Jessica's back to the small house I'd leased.

*

I sat at the small dining table with a mug of tea. I sorted the letters in date order. They went back a good ten years, stopping a couple of months before the letter I'd found by the front door.

"Dear Tom,

How are you and Agnes? I hope you're both as well as I am and that the years are treating you well.

It's been a while since Agnes 'phoned me and I wonder if she's OK. As you know, it's unusual for her to miss our monthly chats and I was getting a bit worried. Please let me know if she's unwell. Perhaps I could pay a visit? I know it's a bit of a meither, what with the train and a bus at each end, but if she's not well …

Anyway, let me know one way or the other – I know your deafness makes using the telephone difficult – perhaps you could write?

Yours, with love,
Jessica"

I hadn't realised that my Grandfather had gone deaf, but why would I be surprised? I took up the next letter.

"Dear Tom

Thanks for your letter. I must say that I was a bit surprised to hear that Agnes has been unwell. Even as a girl, she was never ill – been as fit as a fiddle all her life. Perhaps I really should pay a visit.

Let me know and I'll be on the next train.

I suppose you've told Keith in Canada.
Yours, with love,
Jessica"

I don't recall my Grandfather telling me about Grandma's illness. Would I have forgotten such a thing? Was he losing his memory? I began to wonder, but it was no use worrying now.

The letters continued in this vein over a few months. Suddenly, one of the letters held a shock.

"Dear Tom,

Frankly I'm flabbergasted! Agnes has left you and gone to live with Keith in Canada! After all these years? And without speaking to me? How could she?

What happened? Did you do something to make her leave? Can I contact her in Canada?

Oh! It makes no sense.

You say you were too embarrassed to let me know, but why? We've been such close friends since our early twenties. Ever since – well, you know, before Agnes caught your eye all those years ago.

Oh Tom, you'll have to let her know that I'm asking for her.
Yours,
Jessica"

I too was flabbergasted. Grandma had never come to Canada. What was going on? Had she left him for another man? I know they were getting on a bit, but it's not unheard of, even at their age.

Grandad and Grandma had split up and his pride would not allow him to tell anyone. Not even me, not even Aunt Jessica. I began to feel sorry for him. Living alone all those years, shuffling around this big old house under the grey East Lancashire skies. I wonder if going to the home was a blessing in disguise.

My mind was racing now. What had happened? Why did he tell Aunt Jessica such a lie? What had happened? Where did she go? Where is she now? Perhaps the documents I was to send to Canada held some clues, or even the answer. I couldn't fathom it out. I felt a feeling of despair flowing through my body.

I had to take a break. I poured myself a whisky while thoughts were woven through my mind and then unpicked. What? Why? When? The mystery remained just that.

The next day, I continued my task.

"Dear Tom,

What do you mean she doesn't want anyone to contact her? Not even me? Especially not me? Why would she say that? Oh! I'm terribly worried about her.

Perhaps if you gave me Keith's contact details I can pretend I'm calling my favourite great nephew and somehow move the conversation round to my sister. Maybe that would work.

Yours,

Jessica"

Needless to say, that call never came.

The frequency of the letters tailed off, but were all on the same theme – "Can I contact Agnes?" I guess the replies were always vague.

I wondered if they'd got divorced. I decided that on my return to Canada I'd go through all the documents, perhaps I'd find divorce papers or some other clue.

Meanwhile, I had the house to sort out – I was beginning to feel homesick already. The next day I went to the house and met up with Bill. There was a skip on the drive and I helped him fill it with all the stuff that wasn't needed. Billy said he could upcycle the wooden filing cabinet. I helped him get it into his van.

I parcelled up the documents and went to the main post office. I mailed them to myself. I decided to walk about the town again. It felt strange. Familiarity was cloaked in newness. I phoned Billy and told him I wouldn't be back and I'd see him tomorrow. I drove back to Shorey Bank and walked through the grounds of the madrasah and into Thompson's Park – nothing much had changed there. At the far end, the children's play area had modern equipment and safety surfaces. The boating lake hadn't changed, though the boats looked newer. They were pulled to the edge, upturned and chained together for the winter. Though the park keeper's hut had had a lick of paint recently, it was still that familiar council green, and the red brick building had stood the test of time. The trees were bare and the flower beds dormant. Halfway back, I sat on a bench and pictures of my childhood flowed through my mind like a TV documentary – Gill and Pam, Steve and Bobs, others I couldn't remember. I could see them playing on the swings, or boating, or with a cricket bat and ball, someone's collie outrunning us all. It's funny, when you're a child the sky's not grey and the days are long and sunny. I always thought my childhood was happy and these memories seemed to confirm it.

*

After a couple more weeks the house was sale-ready. Billy had done a good job and I paid him an extra £100 for his efforts. Grandad's garden needed tidying up and I'd do that before I left. I contacted Petty's and told them that I wanted to put the house on the market and that I wouldn't renew the lease on the Shorey Bank property.

Over the next few days I sorted out the front and back gardens. The tools in the old shed weren't of much use, so I bought a spade, fork and rake from B&Q. It was cold, but I made a fire and burned whatever I could. I decided to leave the shed – the new owners could change it if they wanted to. They could have the tools, too, so I put them in the shed.

I took a last look around the back garden then turned towards the house. A power hose and new paint had done the trick. I went in, locking the back door, and went through every room in the house. At the main circuit board, I turned off everything but the lights. The gas and water were also shut off. The front of the house now had what estate agents called "curb appeal" – although I suppose it's *kerb* back over here - the paint was new, the windows clean, the garden was tidy, the wheelie bins stored neatly. I locked up and drove off, for what I thought was the last time.

Back at my rented house I arranged my flight back to Canada. I'd be back on the 20th, just before Christmas. The Skype that night was full of smiles and laughter.

Three days later, I dropped the keys off at the estate agents, went to see Mr Richardson at the practice to place everything in his hands and drove to Manchester Airport.

Christmas and New Year had gone well. It was great to be home. Farzana had kept everything going at the office and nobody there seemed to have missed me. A fleeting thought of retirement crossed my mind. Grandad's house was sold in late March.

*

It was just after Easter and I was just about to set off for the office when the phone rang.

'Mr Peters? Sorry to disturb you so early in the morning, but I'm calling from England. It's about your grandfather's house.'

'Yes. Who is this?'

'I'm Detective Inspector Wiggins from the Lancashire Constabulary.'

The Extra Mile

Ann Ridley

Some stories change you. They entice you, they grip your soul; they never let you go. When Ira saw the flames clutching her beloved book, her school prize for scriptwriting at the age of 14, her screams pierced the sparks shooting into the smoking night. She flew at her mother and clawed her face.

*

'Buy our Fiction of the Month and pick up a free hot drink!'

Marie gritted her teeth. *Who decides this?*

They were everywhere, in neat little Perspex stands, A5 size, a picture of the book cover within, dotted all around the upstairs café. 'Thriller of the month', 'Non-fiction of the month'; artfully arranged piles of books adorning the shelves and windowsills.

Who are the judges in this store? Or is it the publishers' cunning con?

Marie's mission to Orwells was a conscience-laden attempt to order the book she had thrown onto the garden fire. She could not look into her daughter's eyes, could not reason with her.

"Might be out of print now - doesn't really fall into any genre..." The girl with curly green hair stared at the screen. " Not your usual teen fiction or Y. A."

Marie's head swam. "Y. A?"

"Young Adult." The girl was suddenly kindly, having just noticed the marks on her customer's cheek.

"Oh, I wouldn't class her as an adult... not remotely," muttered Marie.

"How about if I do a bit of sleuth-work? Give me your phone number; I'll get back to you in a few days?" The girl caught Marie's despair, her need to be away, into the air.

"I know this book," the girl murmured to Marie's back. "I'll do my best."

Marie walked through her city. She knew it well. She ached for the loss of the quirky, independent bookshops. Only the big boys were left now. The wind blew her down the steep hill to the river.

She turned into a quiet alley. Found herself outside 'All Strung Up'. Drawn in by memories. Gentleness cocooned her. Not your wild rock store, this one. Here was soul. Carpeted. Here were soundproofed booths in which to play instruments, to listen to a special track.

In the far corner, on a stool, a young man bent over an acoustic guitar.

Marie pulled her hair over one side of her face.

He hit a wrong note; looked up with a wry smile.

"Tricky one," she acknowledged.

"You know it?"

"Oh yes, 'Classical Gas' - my – someone I knew used to play it."

"Really?" he paused. "Do you play?"

"Thinking about it." She pretended to study the bewildering array of acoustic guitars hanging above them.

Silence hung.

He put down the guitar and stood beside her.

"Confusing, eh? Look, I work here. Tell me why you want it and you can try a few. Then you can have a think."

An hour later, all she could think about was the light touch of his fingers guiding hers on the strings.

"There's a used one – I think they call them 'pre-loved' these days!" he laughed, "in the store cupboard. I could ask the boss if you can borrow it for a week or three – see how you get on?"

She nodded dumbly.

He shot off.

The plan was agreeable to Mr. Finestra, Manager (for more decades than he liked to remember) of 'All Strung Up'.

A small deposit and – "Here's a First Stages Tutor book. Get your fingers around the chord shapes. I'll ring you in a few days. Is that OK?"

Was that OK? That was very much OK.

The OK 'phone call resulted in an offer to teach the rudiments.

Marie accepted eagerly; how her young pupils would relish singing these songs in the story corner at the end of the boisterous Infant Day! The songs would embellish the stories. Danny assured her that even three chords would provide accompaniment to a bagful of songs. The dread of rainy playtimes would be over.

On his first visit to her house, he smiled softly at Marie's cheek.

"Disappearing," he whispered.

There was a sound in the doorway behind them.

"Oh, Ira – this is Danny. He's come to teach me some guitar chords," said Marie.

"Huh, you didn't say." Ira left the room.

"Teenagers! My kid brother was a pain at that age. We're good mates now though."

Danny attempted to soften the jagged rocks that had suddenly sprung up.

Marie attempted to banish the ageism monster that had crept under the door.

When the Spring Equinox heralded that Marie had mastered enough competence to entrance her five-year-olds, she fretted that her guitar lessons would end. After all, that was The Plan. Four lessons over four weeks.

Now she must buy the instrument and he would go.

Her loneliness hit her like a sheet of ice.

On the fifth week, Marie drove over to Danny's house and not one chord was strummed on a guitar during the hour she spent there.

Marie rang Orwells. In her recent giddiness, the weeks had slipped by and the guilt of Ira's burnt book had dimmed.

"I don't know her name. She promised to find out if it was still in print. She had green, curly hair –"

"Oh, yes - she's on annual leave. I think she's back next week. Gone somewhere with a funny name. Huh – that's her. Have you tried on-line?"

"No match," replied Marie.

"Shall I try?"

Marie gave details of the book. She heard the keyboard rattling.

"Nothing coming up, I'm afraid," said the clipped tones.

"Doesn't matter," Marie slumped, swamped by dismissal.

She was desperate to ring Danny, but realised Ira would soon be home from school.

I must talk with her. I'll make her favourite meal. She's virtually monosyllabic these days; I can't stand it any longer… these long silences...

Ira disposed of the carbonara at breakneck speed. She scraped back her chair.

"Tasty."

"Wait, Ira – please."

"Homework."

"Just a few minutes..." Marie had to steel herself from reaching across the table.

"What?" Sullen, impatient.

"Ira, I've been to Orwells. I've tried to order the book. They think it's out of print. A girl said she'd try to track it down –"

"I know why you did it! Leave it, Mam! It's done, it's over with!" Ira clattered her plate into the sink and ran the hot tap fiercely upon it.

"Just concentrate on your GCSEs for now – then see how you feel –"

"A few paltry O levels won't change my mind!" Ira slammed towards the door. "Have you never heard the phrase – follow your dream?"

"What's this book all about, anyway? It must be pretty weird for you to burn it. You haven't got a cruel bone in your body." Danny lifted Marie's guitar and zipped it into its bag.

Marie sighed. "That's the pity of it all. It's not weird at all. It's a very entertaining, heart-warming story; I enjoyed it myself. It's just – the effect it's had on Ira - and consequently on me..."

Danny took her hand and led her to the settee.

"C'mon – before you go. Free yourself of it, Marie."

"In a nutshell, it's about a young girl who wants to be an actress," Marie smiled wryly, "and all her family are mad keen on this, as her grandfather was an actor – and they all help her."

"Well, it's not hard to guess that Ira has a similar dream," mused Danny, eyes twinkling.

"That's exactly what she said last night! Follow your dream! She has no idea how difficult it is. The uncertainty of it all! And – there's drama school fees." Marie's hand touched her cheek.

"Has she done any acting?" Danny was in problem-solving mode.

"A bit. School plays. She's quite good, actually." Marie felt a rush of pride, which catapulted a surge of guilt.

"Let it drift, then. Roll with the punches!" Danny biffed the air. "Hey - I'll do the music in her first play!"

Marie saw a chasm yawn between them. A chasm of nine years.

He was not a parent. He had few responsibilities. He had not had his heart broken. And that was the crux of it all.

She stood. "I'm going. I want to be in when she gets home from her friend's."

He handed her the guitar case. "There's more, isn't there?"

"Not now, Danny."

"Any point in me talking with her?" he called down the concrete stairwell as she flew to her car.

No point. No point at all. No point in anything. Her knuckles were white as she gripped the wheel and drove out of the bleak estate on the eastern edge of the city. *I shall not cry. I shall be indifferent. I am tired of being discreet. I am tired.*

127

"What are they for, Miss?" Little Robbie stabbed a sticky finger at the symbols on the page.

Marie regarded the skinny, spiky-haired five-year-old leaning against her desk, staring at the letters. At this late stage in the school year, he had not progressed beyond the first book. He was in a constant spin. Life, to Robbie, was fun.

"They are *words*, Robbie. You know, the sounds that we make when we're talking – that's what they look like on the page."

"What's the book for, then?"

"Well, books can take us all over the world..."

"Howzat, Miss? Yer can't ride on 'em." Robbie the comic.

Marie ignored the wit.

He's sharp in some things. Streetwise already. Stand-up.

"You can find out about things you'd like to do, places that are too far away to visit," she continued patiently.

"Got sendy books in my house," he said.

"Sendy books?"

"Pictures of things Mam wants. She says 'I'll send away for it!'" he giggled. "Dad calls them spendy books!"

Before Marie's heart had time to sink, the child's face turned ashen and projectile vomit spewed over her shoes and the surrounding carpet. His wails brought Mrs. Hawkins, the auxiliary, rushing from the toilets where she was supervising the class jesters.

"Keep back! Back! Go and sit in your seats!" Mrs. Hawkins commanded the circle of ghouls who had immediately gathered to gloat. A quick assessment ascertained the boy was still 'with us' as she put it, then with wads of kitchen roll she attacked Robbie's clothes and the teacher's shoes.

"Right, that's the thick off. Now over to the First Aid room, my lamb!" And she hoisted him into her arms and strode out.

"It's orange!" said one, staring at the patch of sick.

"Yella!" insisted another.

"Ugh, Miss, your shoes will be all smelly!" said Annabel Beckonsdale with her nose in the air and her pink hair-ribbon bow waggling in revulsion.

"That doesn't matter. What does matter is that Robbie will feel much better very soon. So think of him tonight before you go to sleep and wish him well."

"I'm thinkin' of him now, Miss!" shouted Jacky Boyd, with his eyes screwed up tightly and his hands bunched together into a little clasp.

"That's very kind, Jacky. Now, I'm going to wash my hands and you, Jacky, can choose a book for story-time, as you've worked so hard today."

Marie sat back on her knees and scrutinised the wet carpet. She had offered to scrub it, as Mrs. Hawkins had taken Robbie home and anyway, why should Ada (Salt of the Earth) Hawkins be landed with these foul tasks? Nor did she want to aggravate the morose nature of the caretaker.

She had scrubbed away her pain, her infatuation.

She had scrubbed away the wound of her broken heart. She had not allowed it to heal since Ira's father's left them. Poor, deluded Oskar; beguiled by an actress.

Three years. Enough.

"Have I got the smell away?" she asked the classroom walls.

Finding an 'Odor-Begone!' spray in the toilets, she lavishly wafted the area, opened the windows, and left a polite note for Lord Morose.

No shoes!

She sat in the car in an old pair of wellies, kept in the store cupboard for rainy playtime duty. She felt compelled to call at Robbie's house on the way home.

The wellies might ease the situation on the doorstep.

A small brown dog snuffled around her wellies as she rang the bell, which, she realised quite quickly, didn't work. The brown dog barked 'Follow me!' and led the way to the back door.

Perhaps that's his role in the family, pondered Marie.

The dog howled and the door flew open.

An astonishingly beautiful woman stared at Marie's face and then at her wellies.

"It went all over your shoes! Yes, I heard! I'm so sorry. The tinker has been wolfing down 'Flying Saucers' again; the sherbet has that effect on him!"

"I thought I'd call on my way home to make sure he was alright." The truth was, of course, that Marie was anxious to discover Robbie's home circumstances.

"Come in; see for yourself!" Robbie's mother ushered Marie into a sunny lounge. Robbie sat, a little prince, clean and glowing in space-ship pyjamas, on the settee, propped up with cushions. He waggled the toast on which he was nibbling.

"'Lo Miss! Won't do that again!"

The two women, virtual strangers, were united in thought. *How could you not love a lad like this?*

"I'm glad you are better. All the children are sending good wishes for you!" his teacher announced.

A glance around the room confirmed her concerns. Not a book in sight.

"I wonder," she ventured, turning to Robbie's mother, "have you a minute to spare?"

"Well, yes – I've been wondering how he's getting on. Come into the kitchen, please."

The kitchen gleamed.

Marie was disconcerted.

"He doesn't seem to see the point of reading, of books…"

"Oh, the house is full of them! They're all up in the girls' rooms. They won't let him in, he wants to draw in them –"

"Ah, yes, daughters -" Marie remembered Robbie chattering about 'the lasses'.

"Three teenagers. Drama crazy. My! the airs and graces they give themselves!" Robbie's mother threw open the kitchen door. "Look!"

Marie gazed out onto what is generally referred to as A Sylvan Glade. Rows of purple garden chairs faced a shed, zinging with gold paint. Bushes of Californian lilac formed a stunning, deep blue backcloth.

"You're gobsmacked, aren't you?" This beautiful woman burst into peals of laughter. "They call it their 'Theatre of Gold'. They perform plays, concerts – for the family, friends, neighbours... they're brilliant really. We all chip in. My man does the techie stuff; I scour the charity shops for costumes. It's a hoot!"

It's more than a hoot; it's a family thing, thought Marie.

She saw a vision of Ira's face. When had she last seen her smile? How she would love this.

"Well, it's lovely to have met you. My name's Dana, by the way," the woman enthused, clasping her by the hand, "but I have to go to work shortly. Robbie's dad will be back soon. The girls will be in, too."

Marie grasped the opportunity. She fished a school letter out of her bag.

"It's Open Afternoon next Thursday. Can you make it? We'll talk more about Robbie's reading – and maybe I could come and see your girls' next play; bring my daughter?"

"Course you can! Tell you what, I'll get my middle girl to take him to the library on Saturday; she's got the most patience."

Marie waved to Robbie as she passed the lounge. He did a grinning 'thumbs up' and returned to 'Dennis and Gnasher' on the screen.

"Kind of you to pop in," said Dana. "Thoughtful."

"I'm glad I caught you before you set off for work," responded Marie.

Dana read the curiosity in Marie's voice.

"I'm a life model," she winked. "For an art class."

Marie drove home, sending up a silent thank you for Robbie's violent reaction to sherbert.

"Wellies, Mam?"

The first friendly overture in weeks.

"Cuppa? You'll never believe the day I've had."

And Marie's daughter listened.

A pair of green size fives crunched up the shingle path.

The name 'Inala' - place of peace – hung above the weather-beaten door.

It creaked open.

"My dear, dear girl! Look at you! How long has it been?"

"Too long, Gran," gasped Curly, squashed by the bear hug. "Not an easy place to get to."

"Ah, the best places are a challenge," teased Gran.

A plate of Anzac biscuits was on the table.

"Billy tea?" asked Gran.

"What else?" joked Curly.

"I've been scouting around since your letter came. Pretty sure it's on that top shelf." They both looked up. "Mostly your mother's books up there. Too high for me now. You'll be able to reach though. Have a browse while I rustle up some tuck."

While Gran Marlee bustled around her kitchen, Curly's fingers slowly traced her mother's books.

It was there. Second from the right. She knew it would be. Safe in this little house.

She stood on tiptoe and eased it out. Still had the cover on; a little tattered, but the inspirational picture was intact. She held it to her chest.

"Found it, Gran!"

"Awesome!" shouted the old lady.

Curly flopped back on the lumpy sofa and gazed around the room. She had spent much of her childhood here and it had barely changed. The old video of 'Crocodile Dundee' was propped against the TV stand. Curly smiled; Gran would be planning to watch it after they had eaten. Gran liked company when she watched this film.

She needed an enthusiastic buddy and Curly always obliged.

Curly's mother had died when she was six and Gran Marlee had raised her, in this spartan wooden bungalow on the wild shingle sweep of Dungeness.

A kangaroo skin water bag dangled from the ceiling; a row of wooden bobbins marched along a shelf and Grandad's old didgeridoo, long silent, occupied a dark corner.

Curly remembered the Dreamtime stories Gran would retrieve from the depths of her spiritual heritage. She had lived near Alligator River in Arnhem Land, Northern Territory and frequently terrified the impressionable young Curly with legends of these huge reptiles.

Unselfishness and the duty of kinship were dominant in Gran's values; she had shelved her grief in order to give her dead daughter's child a loving home.

Curly spent two more days in this fragile landscape.

The pair walked and talked. Gran was unstoppable.

At the top of the Old Lighthouse the wind tossed her question.

"Thought you were going to turn one of your stories into a play?"

"Not much good at dialogue," Curly pulled a face.

"Well, you'll just have to find someone who is!" No-nonsense advice.

Gran took her to see Credence Paddick whose arthritic knees had been eased by a visit from four medicinal leeches that Gran had located in the gravel pits.

"Kinda like your Gran's bushcraft!" chuckled Credence, rubbing her knees appreciatively. She squinted at Curly. "Long way to come for a book."

"Worth it, though," the girl answered seriously.

The green boots paused at the gate.

"I promise I won't leave it so long next time!"

"Mind you keep writing!"

The old lady turned away hastily, hating goodbyes.

A note in Ira's bold capitals lay on the kitchen table when Marie returned from school.

'RING ORWELLS.'

The girl with the curly green hair answered.

"I've got the book you wanted. It's an old copy –"

"Wonderful! Thank you so much. Where did you find it?"

"Ira, will you come with me – to Orwells? Meet this girl who has found a copy of your book?" Marie wanted to add 'to thank her', but felt that was a step too far at the moment. Let that happen naturally.

Ira nodded.

Curly was busy with a customer. She recognised Marie and indicated an empty table in the café, below the stained glass window.

Marie and Ira sat, waiting.

Why am I nervous? Please, Ira, be nice to this girl. She's gone out of her way to help. She's truly an 'extra mile' person.

Marie felt the future was held in this moment.

The sun glinted onto the green curls as the book was laid on the table before Ira.

On the cover was a vibrant picture of a family performing a play in Shakespearean costume in their garden.

Ira's fingers hovered over each actor in turn.

"They're there; they're all there... the family," she breathed.

Marie gripped the table. *This has been it all along. It's not just about the acting. It's the family. She has loved this family. This is what she's longed for. And I threw this family into a fire... How did I miss this?*

"Look, I've got some shopping to do. Can I pay and leave you two to . . .?"

Curly grinned and waved Marie away.

"Nothing to pay. Worth it. We have stories to tell."

Remnants of a Penknife Phallectomy

Johnny O

The Day Dick L...

A Cautionary Tale for Boys ana ...

...very, Saturday morning

...alingalingalingalingalingalingalingalingalingalingaling...!...
' Thock! Thut!

...cked the top of the grubby, beaten-up old alarm clock wit..
...ich it duly did, after several maladroit and badly-aimed slaps
...d pulled his arm back under the duvet.

...he alarm clock for half past fucking eight? It's ...
...st the pillows on the other side of the bed.
...o un... set it from the week,' Kevin mumble...'

...n my ears,' she complained. 'I can't sleep r
...hat attitude,' he grumbled drowsily. 'Stop

...de awake now.' She stared at the ceiling
...hair skewed over the right-hand side of he...
...ed up and fell right back again. She brushed it
...tion at the ceiling. 'Nope, I'm definitel...
...ned to the crumpled mound beside '
... find a face or at least some h
...ne a muffled jackhammer ur
...k the duvet on her side and sat up with a jerk. It was preferable to
noted. 'Unbelievable!' She slid her slim, pale legs off the side of the
unny slippers, wondering as she looked down at her feet why she'd
r of times she'd tripped over or trodden on those stupid floppy ears and
... of these days she'd be found at the bottom of the stairs doing her most
a gammadion or something even worse composed of lower-case Greek
...ould end up recording a verdict of 'Death By Bunnies'. She stood up,
...d, and smoothed out her satin nightie, then padded across the bedroom,
...d jeans strewn across the carpet, and made her way to the bathroom. She
...the morning, but today the assorted shower products in the clip-on soap
...' at her nettled her, reminding her as it did of the prat she'd left in bed.
...ve a long, relaxing soak in the bath, and turned the hot tap full on. Then
bath bombs in so as to well and truly stink the place out for when
...ing mischievously. She slipped the nightie off and slid into the tub.
...our and a half later when she awoke with a start and a noseful of soapy
...lf dry and put her nightie and slippers back on, then carefully, feet on
...ent down to the kitchen.
...t, are you, Catface?' she commented to the absent feline, noticing the
...r as it did every time the cat exited. 'Well, I'll feed you whenever you
flap were two scuffed brown and orange trainers, one with a broken lace,
...ide which looked as though they hadn't so much been placed there as

                                    ﹏ue t.
                            ﹏ner Jamie Oliver
                         ﹏ankfully closed, from which p
                      ﹏ grey tongue of kebab meat. *Hmmm, thou*
            ﹏ego *man is in aid of. But a beer mat from The Pit – that*
         ﹏*ght*… The kettle pinged at the same time as there came a loud .
﹏om: *The clown's up,* she thought as she poured boiling water up to the Bodu
﹏ere, slotting the press back on top… *And,* she continued her reasoning, *he cl*
﹏*ies or whichever other god-awful takeaway after that. But the box is closed, s*
﹏*a taxi – hence no notes, just coins – and he didn't stay up to finish it when h*
﹏*netime between four and half past, I'd estimate.* She indulged in a satisfied lit
﹏lations, then frowned at the realization that she had been calculating how r.
boyfriend was. After he'd said he wouldn't be back late: '*I'm just going for a* .
he lads after work, babe. I won't be late, OK?' Every time. Every bloody time.
﹏*auuuughhhhh!! What the fuck!? Fuckfuckfuck!! What the…!? Aaoohhhh!*'
llocks!' Sarah dropped her favourite Snoopy mug, scowled with chagrin
he bathroom bawl to blame, and nonetheless scurried up the stairs.

        11:23 when Kevin Craven awoke suddenly, for no apparent reason, and it
        after that, after determining to attempt another hour or so in bed, that he felt
        ﹏ go to the toilet, a sharp pain in the hardened, distended bolus of his ﹏
        ball of high-pressure urine was already trying to force its wa﹏ ﹏
        He leapt out of the bed, ran toward the door, tripp﹏﹏ ﹏
        ﹏d cannoned headlong into the wall, co﹏﹏﹏
        ﹏s-relief woodcarving of a ﹏﹏﹏
        ﹏ectly into Ke﹏﹏'
        ﹏to ﹏

        ﹏s-to-do-free Saturday morning but for the fact that he be﹏
        ﹏at at the other end of him he had partially pissed himsel!
        wet patch on his blue-and-white striped boxers. Another s﹏
        he convulsed into a hunched gamma-like semiverticality an﹏
        m as quickly as possible, in what could only be described a﹏
        tching his floody, bloody nose and the other hand clamp﹏
        grunting insensibly, like some awful pantomime Quasimo﹏
        ﹏g all the wrong fluids from all the wrong places. *What a ho*﹏
        to himself inside his battered and slightly sick, woozy head
        ﹏pen. *Well, at least it can't get much worse from here.* He h﹏
        ﹏e lid, turned and pulled his dripping boxer shorts off
        ﹏eeling a long scarf of toilet roll from its holder with such a v﹏
        ﹏r tape about his feet. He gathered the pink papery coils up
        ﹏e, feeling his eyes bruising and blackening already as he﹏

...urine, between his legs and b...
...was... well, a what?... it was a... just a hole, just a... a
...ian anything. An oval hole no more than a centimetre long ar
bare, featureless hole. An opening. The end of a tube
usculature of any kind. Just a hole. It wasn't even a hole that
wasn't a lady hole. It was just a hole. Just below the arc of
head of a pubic clearing – *no penis, no scraggy scrotum*, ju
t white flesh which nauseated Kevin just to look at. There w
ll (most of this was draining from his nose, bent over at this
otten about his face), just a bare patch and a hole. He stuck
ce and dug and grubbed around its waxy smoothness fran
it cause his – maybe, just maybe, retracted – genitalia to be
speration he wiggled and wormed his index finger in the
sed? – nearly to his second knuckle, pulled it out with
sickening plastic hole in a sickening, floury-white, pubic
...evin's gorge rose up his oesophagus abruptly, leapt ev
...et of water, bypassing any restraint reflex, and a stream of se
meat vomit erupted through his mouth and nose, burning through th
spattered, and sprayed by the toilet paper wad all over his knees and t
It was at this precise moment that Sarah burst into the bathroon

'*Kevin!* What the fuck are you doing!?' Sarah's voice was twist
with reproach; her face the same, like one of those contorted theatre masks
'I... it's, *guh...*' Kevin gurgled, his pallid face still slopped with
eyes welling with big, brimming, uncontrollable tears, which gushed forth l
and wound rivulets through his filthy, putrid face as he sobbed, burbling. Sarah
as far as confusion, bordering even on concern – though he did have a tender
into sticky wickets entirely of his own design, and she wasn't prepared
yet.

'What have you done?' – *or more like what haven't*
appened?' she asked more tenderly, kneeling in front ... starting
nit from his chin and upper lip with the expensi... wipes from h
'It's gone!' he squeaked between blub... And he subsided
ot once more.
'What's gone, Kevin?' she ...hough she could feel the irrita
the nape of her neck ...ulder blades, a tiny bristling bug skip
'What are you ... shuffled over to the bath, thankful now
though ...ked the malodorous tang, and twisted
... n, let's wipe you down and get you in
... as she could muster, suppress
...on sign in her head, was:
and wiped the vomit
...ew carpet, less
... to wear
toil

...would no
...the emblematic arc
...puke slarted about Kevin's
...kled cluster galaxy of crimso
...ggrieved, and turned still sc
...ed closer, scrutinizing the bri

,ec

She ti

ound emerge

't laugh. Don't la

is gaze ever so slightly,

d his mouth and looked down,

said very quietly without looking up.

n queried, baffled, though she could feel the

ary smile. She bit her lip again. 'What d'you say?'

s gone,' he repeated in the most intimate whisper that cam

?' she sniggered, immediately attempting to disguise it as

h'm! What d'you mean, gone?'

's gone,' he stated, gesturing limply at the wrists, hand

d her neck between his parted thighs her first-

ne Penis.

ouldn't help smiling to herself as

in her *second* favourite Sn

). She stirred the n

't help smiling.

about it.   seemed so uni

al   c, about it all. After all, it hadn't

us some gruesome form of torture. No, there was nothing gru

ugh Kevin undoubtedly would, clearly *did*, disagree; but it was almost as

d away by magic. Or left of its own accord. Just dropped off and left. And tl

und, was what really tickled her about the whole incident. It had taken ev

bre of her restraint to guide her shell-shocked boyfriend from the toilet seat t

wn the toilet, give the carpet a prefatory scrubbing, scour the tiling, the skirti

n cabinet; and repair his pissy boxers to the washing machine, without burs

s.

Did that make her a terrible person? Or was it still *schadenfreude* if

v hurt – and aside from his state of temporary trauma it seemed he was

ain – and if it wasn't Misfortune, if he did, as he did, so karmically deserve i

yway. Either because he was out getting drunk, or because when he did re

'd withhold sex as punishment. Or he himself was incapable. For whate

impotent, premature. Maybe Mr. Cheney – *his* stupid moniker, she always

iming of members puerile – had finally got sick of it all and decided to up

ould be fitting. But obviously ludicrous. Though she instinctively slippe

nickers at the thought; no, it was reassuringly crevicitudinous...

ink my nose might be broken,' Kevin mumbled as he shuffled in through

in his dressing gown – Sarah retracted her hand quickly and resumed slurpir

slumped onto a stool. 'And there's a clown face imprint

l, never mind that,' Sarah consol

se is brok

the fifties or
again. He mu:
details, *now w*
dick, and dickle.
 'You kn(
 'What? S(
at the notion, whicl.
Kevin had come to t.
 'I really think
 'What, Cheney
Sarah, miming throu
tabletop.
 '\'
un~'

.rs .
.:frained .
.x *up.* And eve.
.uld think of better w(
..ing sternly out of the wind\
, .igh she wasn't sure whether it w
.. she believed it when she thought of it.
.nclusion.
.ve left home,' he said again, 'as it were.'
off and hopped out the door after Catface, did he?' quip.
.otions with animated finger-skipping gesticulations across t..

ow...' he began, and paused mid-sentence: 'Wait, *what?* The r
'tpboard, all snuggled in with the warm towels again.'
ked, one eyebrow raised.
replied impatiently: 'I just came down from ther
she indicated the door – 'the cat must be r
~laimed, growing hysterical as he !
'tchen to the open catflap. 'M'
'stles of the doormat, sc'

you'll injure your~
.t He's di~appe~
as though '
.tt hole at t'
' with

...u I ne
..t:; we should appr(

.. ine Pursuit, Saturday afternoon

 Mrs. Florence Delilah O'Houlihan was a remarkable woman for a numbe.
amongst these was that she was alive. At one hundred and eleven years of a
.t her husband by forty four years, almost as long as they had been marrie(
.ng over the one hundred mark and disappearing over the horizon with a cheery
.t that she should have picked up a model forty years younger at that point, her .
.t he may just have lasted her long enough. But, she admitted, it would probably
'dered appropriate at the funeral, or even the wake, at which she got very dr(
.as frowned upon by some of her more prudish friends. Who were also now de.
.t all four of her sisters and both her brothers. She had outlived four of h(
' her eighty five year old daughter Millicent resided in the room adjoining hers
.t Home for the Elderly and sometimes Florence had to assist her in getting u|
.rs. No, Florence O'Houlihan was going nowhere – she was staying right .
.s to two other remarkable things about her. She wasn't as young as she us~d '
hundred and eight, and capering all over the nursing home kee~'
' nurses busy trying to keep up. But after twistin~ '
le at the summer lawn party – which ''' '
' – she had been advised bv tt-
'entary, hobby. S~ '

. ̤ad nobody r̤
. ̤ne hundred and eighty si̤
̤ay window. She wouldn't let anybc̤
̤ ̤ her seat. Even if she wasn't sitting there. Ev̤
̤ ̤er many grandchildren, great-grandchildren, great-great-grar̤
̤ ̤great-grandchildren.

It was from this seat, or the bench on the lawn on fine summer da̤
Nothing happened on or around Willow Grove without her knowledge. She saw
̤ when she saw young Sarah Hollister coming up the driveway, with her dopy
tow, who looked like he'd lost an argument with a pantechnicon, she already ̤
picions as to the purpose of their visit.

'Come in, dear, come in,' she said, waving them over and patting the a̤
'ow as the young Catalunyan Nurse Gil Vila showed them into the day room.
̤ You too, Kevin,' she continued with nosy urgency, and without pausing a ̤
̤ou been doing, boy? Black eyes, bloody nose? And...' – she adjusted her spec̤
̤ closer, and Sarah smiled – 'is that a clown face imprinted on your forehe̤
̤d you manage that, you bally idiot? Honestly, you really are the most ̤
̤n at times. Lord alone knows what would have become of this country if y̤
̤

̤e would have elaborated in this strain at length, as she often did, in her a̤
̤e some formidable Wodehousean aunt, but Sarah mercifully int̤
boyfriend's account:
̤. O'Houlihan...'
̤nce, dear, Florence.'
̤nce... ah...' Sarah ̤ ̤ ̤ ̤perience proving a dusty scrubla̤
such oc̤ ̤ ̤ ̤ith a rather... ah... *delicate* enquiry. ̤
̤een, ah... abandoned, as it were, by... e̤
̤uttered on, but Florence dove in unflinchir̤

̤ur penis has left home and have I seen i̤

̤s, I have,' Florence state̤ ̤t was yours; there can't be too many
̤und at will.'
̤n was this? *Where* was t̤ ̤ forward on the edge of his stool,
̤nce's hand. 'Is he OK?'
̤ seemed fine, dear, fine,' s̤ ̤roking his hand. 'Reminded ̤
̤nostalgic smile flickered mo̤ ̤s – 'you're quite the ̤
̤eel it right now, I must say, ̤ping, hands e̤
̤ps.
̤ast we've got a sighting. D̤
̤er hand, then turning ba̤

̤e insisted ̤
̤An̤

— anc

.y weekend – c

y little man he is; he p.

he's even had the brass neck tc

...gh Victorian ceiling and clenched his jaw, but

...os and glared a warning as if to say: *Don't you dare! If*

k and use it again you'll know what's good for you and keep y.

· and slumped further, like a naughty schoolboy, but remained s

finished with him, and I remember sitting in here with another p.

...ble fighting its way out of the coiled tentacles of the kraken of s

'd nine. And I watched the lane to see if the paperman was abo...

nd there he was!' she concluded triumphantly.

...sked quizzically.

'lorence corrected her. 'What would h

'd nothing, feeling fool...

rence ...

...on behind

...rooks like he's go.

...was in town, in a heated argumen.

...y of parking, or 'embedding', as the mana...

...e bus concourse; Sarah was extracting said Corsa; ...

...assumed the mantle of Penis Envoy – it was the most peculia

...arjorie Watkins turned up for her Monday morning shift at the muniti...

less; she wouldn't be doing that again in a hurry. Primarily on account ...

needed a bra again, much less in a hurry – was in the news kiosk enquiri...

Cheney had caught.

'Well,' she reported after Kevin and Sarah had assembled in the doc...

directly opposite the bus station, 'serendipity is on your side, lad. It wou...

friend had to wait 'til one thirty, just a few minutes ago, to catch a bus into th...

the two-two-five, which as you know takes a rather circuitous route via th...

Saturn and takes just over an hour and a half if the traffic is clement,' – as if ...

meteorological condition – 'and it's the weekend; so he can't be too far ahead

'oy; take the motorway and put your foot down and we'll catch the blighter in n...

d Arth's fictitious friend was wont to proclaim: *the game's afoot!*'

As he cannoned the Corsa down the motorway Kevin tried n...

...usness of his jeans, which still gave him a queasy ...

...ness. He tried to focus on the hurtling tarmac ahe...

... to the pedals made him notice the moti...

than before, looser than before ...

nd other amputees exr...

...sensation of th...

d back ...

. There. It was t.
, as that after having .
.calp feel cold and expose.
.ought he glanced at the rear-view
np. He sighed, offered a coarse imprecat.
.arder on the accelerator, fighting the urge to
y skidded over vibratory white lines. In the b?

The transport information clerk w·   .ily in his swiver v.
glassed-in office-cum-bureau, slurpin·   .stic beaker of watery brow.
muck trying, unsuccessfully, to p·   .en made from only the finest
beans, and struggling to think of a   .uries, *d-i-blank-blank-blank*,
reverie was torn open by a screeching a.   s Alecto, Megaera, and Tisiph
foulest of vengeful moods – though since i.   oorn and had spent all his life
box he himself would have been unaware o1   .-·. He snapped back
witness a silver Corsa hurtle past his roadside v.   .-ilously hard
next corner, and disappear down the sidestreet to the
'Bloody idiots!' he muttered with disdain, then
.9 semi-divine inner numen, he filled in the blanks – *I*
°-satisfied air. He treated himself with a doughnut   .r v.
Thirty seconds later, when he was *sure* th·   .structin₅
' a *symbolism*, he was again shaken ·   ' ittle World .
.nging of glass panels at the c1·   .-esk. He sco.
over to the slatted windo·   .·is slouch, '
the hyperanimated f·   .·is m

.Now sur, ii you .'ll jus' ca!
the problem, then?' He noticed that the strange man seemed to be wearin
make-up, for his visage was that of a comic villain, or some such; alab:
about the eyes, a crooked, bloodied nose, and, most peculiar of all, what
sort of clown-face insignia stamped right in the middle of his fo
prominent brows. 'Are yew lookin' fur the theaytur?' he enquired wit|-
sum of yure friends 'ave bin through today.' His accent ranged wildly
encompassing almost all 400-odd miles of the south coast as well as
moors and rugged coves of the West Country, via Bath and Bristol, and
into the south of Wales: a Hancock of an accent.
    'No, I'm not looking for the...' Kevin cried, then paused a
comment struck him: 'Friends? What, like... 'theatre types'? I'm loc
been a dick in here today?' His speech picked up pace, so that he blur
as one word, and repeated: '*Ha'y'seen'nydicks?*'
    'Ho, sur,' the clerk laughed; 'oi see plenty o' dicks in 'ere o
'ave to corl 'em Sur, Madam. But what oi'd loik to say, ho ho...'
    'No, no, no, no!' Kevin ululated in frustration, wringing his h
foot to the other uselessly. 'I mean an actual *dick*. A penis. You m
'theatre type'.' *Or whatever the hell it is that you're thinking.*
    'O-*ho*, oi see, sur,' – he was determinedly relaxed – 'well, no·
    'Yes, yes! What?' Kevin hopped excitedly. *How the hell di·*
    ·· ··- ·h--·t? What did you think I was thinking ab·

, the clerk corrected himself in his u

was it.'

e's gone to Bristol?' Kevin felt a reassuring hand on his arm

caught up with him. He continued, calmer: 'Or… when *is* th

 io, sur. The only coach to Bristol on a Saturday leaves at noi

ied, to Kevin's visible, and audible, relief. 'No, oi think 'e

!! Thanks!' Kevin made to depart when the clerk said, for i

cy:

ut sur! Sur!' Then, *lente*: 'Sur, oi think 'e was doin' sum sl

ik Street. The next train to Bristol to moy knolledge isn't '

n 'ower.'

s brilliant! Thanks!' Kevin clapped his hands in joy, and t

O'Houlihan go to the station and see if he's already there· I

a'd been able to ···

. consent ·

oub of weekenu

·e, taking Sarah by the

sedately along the City Wa.

a lovely view of the Gardens in

, man,' reflected the clerk when the·   ·eu. 'Oi

·bowt.' And he settled himself dow·   ·o the claggy prol

·s.

·McDonald's drew blanks, and puzzled frowns; but upon entering

·nexed to the Marlborough Centre, Kevin struck lucky with

·untered.

·this dick in here before, yes,' squeaked the girl, whose slapped-on-to-th·

sis make-up rendered her face even more garish and *outré* than Kevin's own

·i on his credit card. Now what did he buy? Oh yes, he bought a can of Dr Pepper

·like for a Ken doll or something. He didn't want a bag, 'cause he left wearing it.

·ally – he looked quite *dashing*.' She giggled girlishly. Kevin glowered at her

·ynicism, emanating disparaging mind-rays which failed utterly to penetrate

·t leaden foundation, and strode out of the store.

·iis is parading about the town in a trenchcoat, like he's fucking Columbo!

tly – he mouthed the word in silent mockery – *like some fucking gumshoe*

films noirs Sarah likes. He barged through a crowd of meandering idiots.

·ed with wry, unleavened humour. He looked at his watch. Ten minutes!

·i couple of hundred yards from Central Station. He could still make it.

·back. But what would he do when he found him? *Rebuke him? Plead*

·nd shove him back under denim? He hadn't thought that far ahead.

sees how desperate I am, sees how much I need him, how I c··· ·

·come back to me? He's bound to forgive me and·

·e standing vigil outside the main·

·· down, resting his han·

·i th·

⸺ⲟⲛ t seen him come through here,' ⸺
⸺ where can he be?'

⸺ply. 'If he's anything like me – and I'c
⸺ be waiting in the bar.' And with that
⸺ station façade.

⸺ ⲟⲩld high⸺ aulted, ornately decorated, ceramic til⸺
⸺ⲟⲛ a bar when C⸺tral Station had been built, it had serve
⸺g room perhaps, but it wa⸺ spacious and, for once, sensibly deemed
⸺ⲟⲩt and replace'. So it was conve⸺ed into a bar. It was through the front
⸺ⲁⲉ Flying Scotsman that Kevin came full t'lt, and halted abruptly, like the villain
⸺ ⲟy the hero's ray gun. The barman, channel-hopping on the plasma screens above the bar,
ⲓⲟoked up from his multi-buttoned remote control for a brief moment, and gawped slackly.

There, not six yards away, was Mr. Cheney, trenchcoat and all, collar up, looking dashing on his bar stool with a Singapore Sling. Three further Singapore Slings sat drained before him on the pink granite bar top, charged, like the trenchcoat and his train tickets, to the account of Mr. Kevin Ignave Craven. He turned to Kevin and they contemplated one another, motionless, eye to eye, as if in thrall, for some ten, twenty seconds, before the announcement for the two forty for Plymouth burbled over the Tannoy, breaking the cantrip; whereupon he hopped casually from the bar stool, nodded his head in a genial fashion, turned, and strolled, purposefully but still casually, out of the door and across to Platform 9, where the train was waiting. Kevin dangled limply i⸺
middle of the bar like a forgotten marionette, hollow and shell-shocked.

'*Ah!* I used to love this when I was a kid!' the barman cheere⸺
settling on a channel:

'Maybe tomorrow, I'll want to settle down;
Until tomorrow, I'll just keep moving on... '

Flightless Birds

Sara Waymont

It's no use going back to yesterday, because we were all different people then.

Imagination is the only weapon in the war against reality, but it gets slowly kicked out of you, one booted bill and overdue office deadline at a time. As a child, everything is possible. Become an adult, spend half of your life shuttling backwards and forwards in a vibrating metal box and your whole world shrinks down until it becomes just two seemingly endless lines of white and red.

Headlights and tail-lights.

Day in, day out.

Accelerate. Brake. Accelerate. Brake.

Brake.

Brake.

Break.

Wait.

Break, breaking, broken.

The engine stops.

The engine starts.

The same mundane shit, over and over again; your own, personal, Groundhog Day.

It takes all the running you can do, just to keep in the same place.

This morning is cold and clear. The sky is velvet, heavy with sleep, laden with twinkling stars. A hint of pale blush pink is just beginning

149

to appear as a thin sliver along the horizon. Frost blankets the world in silver and silence, sparkling with promise, street lights glinting off of the rime.

As I scrape the ice from my car with an old CD case, numb fingers fumbling with the task, I'm rocked by the overwhelming desire to turn right and not left at the end of the road. Instead of going to work, I could drive out into the glistening countryside with my shaggy old dog in the seat by my side and go walking during the magical hush of pre-dawn.

It would be peaceful there, in the midst of all the fallow farmer's fields. The only sound the soft scrunch, scrunch, scrunch of frozen grass crackling beneath my feet and the gentle padding of my mongrel's footsteps. A startled pheasant might suddenly burst from the hedgerow and momentarily shatter the tranquillity with its panicked cries, tempting my hound to give chase, but otherwise all else would be still.

Out into the darkness we would wander, each rejoicing in the other's company, contented by the simple pleasure of just being together. I'd throw a stick and she'd bring it back, panting and smiling with her tongue lolling to one side. When I'm with her and she's with me, we need nothing more to complete us.

Her heart and my heart are very old friends.

Once upon a time, there was a lonely princess who lived in a tiny room, high up in a tower. Some people envied her position of comfort, but what they didn't know was that she was very much alone. Her only friend in the world was a stumpy grey pony, whose legs were too short and whose belly was too big. The princess would stand at her window, looking down at the little horse and the pony would whinny up to the princess, urging her to leave the confines of her prison.

One day, after many years of waiting for just such a chance, the princess managed to escape her captivity, by calling out to a passing eagle. The noble bird took pity on the princess in her gilded cage and bade her take hold of his talons so that he might carry her down to the wild grasslands where the pony lived.

Finally liberated from her tower, the princess thanked the eagle and together she and her equine companion travelled out into the mysterious and wild land of...

Essex.

It's full of people and the roads are always busy, even if you leave at the crack of sparrow's fart.

I'm fed up of having to wake up two hours before I'm due to start work, just so that I can get going while it's still reasonably quiet. I'm utterly sullen as I finish de-icing my car and I'm positively cranky when I cram my aching body into the driver's seat and switch my brain into autopilot.

I drive down the hill and onto a quiet country road, my lower back protesting all the way. Human beings were not designed to sit on their arses all day long. We aren't supposed to spend the best years of our lives stuck inside sanitised buildings, struggling to make enough money for our ends to barely meet, but the Deity of the Modern World demands it. Make the money to buy the things. Sit at the computer, press the buttons, click the mouse, say 'yes' to the boss, say 'yes' to the overtime, be pleased with your generous twenty eight days of annual leave.

Twenty eight days to be your own master.

Twenty eight days to be yourself.

Enjoy what you do and you'll never work a day in your life. For the rest of us, the brutal truth of reality; work every day whether you enjoy what you do or not, because you weren't born rich and you aren't likely to win the lottery any time soon.

I switch the radio off and allow my mind to wander.

How do you run from what's inside your head?

My daydreams, at least, are still my own.

...together the princess and the pony have adventures.

They battle savage monsters, help the needy and liberate the oppressed, for the princess is also a warrior. They travel to distant lands where there is no grass, only sand, where there is no sun, only rain, where it is so cold that the land is permanently mantled by snow and where it is so hot that it is only safe to travel overnight.

Together the princess and the pony have known war and deprivation and they have tested themselves over and over again. Until, at long last, their path takes them by a familiar route and they finally return home.

When they arrive at the wild grasslands where the pony used to graze, they find the meadows scorched and black. The tower that had once been the princess's bridewell is broken and ruined. Coming back from afar to the place they thought they knew, the princess and the pony realise that many things have changed.

But, today, after a journey long, long, long, and much searching, the princess and the pony will stand face-to-face with the corrupt source of the destruction; a wild eyed witch with hooked nose and wicked tongue.

This dark enchantress and agent of chaos is known as...

My boss.

Her face imposes itself upon my musings entirely unbidden.

I know I shouldn't, but I hate her.

I'm sure that outside of work she's a positively kind and perfectly loveable person.

Well, I'm not *sure,* if truth be told, but I'm open to the possibility, even though nothing about her workplace demeanour suggests it. Her voice is shrill and her eyes are crazy. Even when she's trying to be nice, she can't help but come across as slightly unhinged. Most of the time, she wears an expression that can only be described as a sneer, as though there's a bad smell right under the tip of her nose that she just can't shift.

Every day I have to grit my teeth, both physically and metaphorically, and summon up the courage to survive another eight hours in her odious presence.

The effort feels truly heroic.

Through the soundless backroads I drive, contemplating the awaiting horrors that another day of micromanagement will bring, with just the whoosh of the heater blowing hot air for company.

I wonder if it might be worth tugging the steering wheel sharply to the left and driving myself into a ditch. I contemplate how much more exciting my day would be if I wrapped my vehicle around a tree. Right now, these ideas feel like a perfectly logical way to liven up my existence.

That's what a career in corporate bullshit will do to you.

Perhaps, deep down inside, we all still carry the longing for adventure, the hope that something special will end the monotony and free us from the prison of routine.

Does anybody else notice how much of their lives are stolen?

Is that why people take gap years?

Or embark upon a midlife crisis?

On days like today, for a short while at least, I can still make myself believe that anything might be possible, but the closer I get to work, the more the sensation fades and the more enticing a high-speed car-crash begins to seem.

...and the princess and the pony ride into the Forest of Forgetting, following the Stream of Dreams That Were Lost....

By the time I hit the motorway the feeling of possibility is almost entirely gone, just an echo of an echo of an echo whispering soft and sad from somewhere forgotten and remote.

Every now and again the child inside of me bridles at the loss.

She thrashes and kicks.

Why?

Why is this my life?

What happened to the Looking Glass and to pretend and make believe?

... the princess and the pony can feel the wicked sorcery here.

The air is thick with evil spells that seek to steal their memories and harden their hearts to one another. Under the hoary boughs of the ancient oaks time becomes meaningless and thoughts become as tangled as the twisting roots that criss-cross the stony path.

The princess had heard it said that those who stayed too long beneath the trees never leave. They forget whatever dreams they once had, abandon whichever path they were on and settle for a life beneath the leaves that goes nowhere and achieves nothing. They die, never having truly lived, giving themselves to the growth of the trees and the eternal expansion of the hungry Forest.

But the princess and the pony are breakers of enchantments.

Shaking off the sorcery, the princess draws her sword and prepares to do battle with…

The mortgage.

That's why I put myself through this.

Get on the property ladder and you will never get off. It will hold you fast from the moment you sign your life away to the day that you retire.

If you're lucky, that is.

If you're fortunate enough to continue being able to pay.

If nothing goes wrong with your job or your health or the economy.

And when you finally fulfil that monstrous debt, you'll be old and grey and wondering what it all meant. Sure, you'll have a roof over your head, but they'll take that away anyway to pay your bills when you need to go into care. Of course, you'll have escaped the trap of renting, but there aren't any pockets in a shroud and you aren't fitting that two bed semi in your coffin when they plant you.

First comes the mortgage, then the shrinking of options, next the loss of opportunities and finally the abandoning of ambition.

I've let her down, that small girl with braids past her waist and big ideas in her brain. I've become part of the machine, the ever-turning wheel, more cog than person.

I'm playing my part, but is it really the part I want to play?

....the princess sees the doppelgänger and the pony shies and rears. She hadn't expected to meet herself here and she wonders what its appearance means.

The creature looks just like her, but with empty eyes and sunken cheeks and from it exudes a rank stench. Hopelessness rolls off of the creature in waves, more potent even than the smell. Its skin is pale, like the grave, and covered with a damp and poisonous sheen. The princess has heard tales of such fiends, created by the trees to subdue any who resist them.

The shadow-twin lurches forward and reaches for the princess, with bony fingers outstretched and a silent scream distorting the familiar features.

But the princess is strong and the pony is bold. She urges her sturdy mount onwards with her heels and together they charge...

Onto the dual carriageway.

This is the part of the journey I despise the most.

Start. Stop. Start. Stop.

Brake. Accelerate. Brake. Accelerate. Brake.

Brake.

Brake.

Break.

Wait.

Break, broken, broke.

I grew up being told that I could do and be anything that I wanted. It turns out that I can do and be only what the God of Family Fortune and Privilege has decreed.

With ten million in the bank I could be anything.

With ten pounds fifty and an overdraft I'm reduced to a wage slave, toiling for my next pay cheque. A serf tied to the humdrum reality of nine-to-five just to stay alive.

Though the work isn't back-breaking, it's mind-numbingly dull.

Now manual labour is something to aspire to; tilling fields for a week during a holistic wellbeing retreat that gets me 'off-grid'. Give me a spoon to whittle and all of my problems will be solved, my soul will be healed.

Am I better off than my predecessors?

If we make the measure in material wealth, then undoubtedly I am.

I have more technology; gadgets to wash and cook and clean. I have plentiful food in my oversized fridge and Netflix and Prime and the highest possible broadband speed. I have new clothes and a car, a mobile phone with WhatsApp and Facebook and virtual friends. I pay the obligatory gym membership, so that I can Insta all of my #GOALS. I've acquired every basic accoutrement of Twenty First Century living

157

and, on the face of things at least, I seem to be playing the game equally as well as most.

Do I have too much choice or just too much time to think?

Am I the epitome of a First World Problem?

...the princess swings her vorpal blade and snicker-snack the beast's head is parted from its neck.

A soft wind comes rustling through the leaves and a sibilant whisper sighs:

"Beware Responsibility, my girl

The jaws that bite, the claws that rend.

Beware the Nine-to-Five, and shun

The frumious Commute without end."

Victorious, the princess wheels her mount and cries, "O frabjous day! Callooh! Callay!"

And chortles in her joy.

Beheaded, the limp and lifeless body of the manxome foe falls to...

The tarmac.

It's cracked and uneven, like my heart.

Both have seen better days.

Small stones scrunch under the wheels as I turn into the empty carpark, reverse into a poorly delineated bay, barely outlined with flaky white paint, and come to a shuddering stop.

Turn the key, shut down the ignition.

Shut down the spark.

Shut down.

I'm momentarily disorientated.

When the engine dies, its white-noise drone is replaced by the bass hum of trains and cars outside my windows, reverberating through the glass; sound that is felt as much as heard.

My right knee throbs, protesting the repetition of start, stop, start, stop.

Brake. Accelerate. Brake. Accelerate. Brake.

Brake.

Brake.

Break.

Wait.

Break, broke, broken.

The sky brightens, glowing soft peach and pale grey-blue. Skeletal trees, stripped bare by the season, reach up into the ether, clawing at the uncaring sky. Gnarled trunks become twisting branches and needle-thin twigs, like the bristles of a witch's upturned broom.

And they remind me.

They remind me of my carefree youth.

They remind me of how it felt not to have to be anywhere or do anything or pay anyone.

They remind me of the visceral reality of simply being able to just *be*.

...all mimsy are the wispy trees, ancient weeping willows bowing low over the Stream of Hopes Not Realised, but still the princess and the pony continue on.

One foe is vanquished, but the greater evil still remains; the harridan who commands absolute obedience, crushes all rebellion and denies any freedom of thought; the loathsome striga who feeds upon oppression and steals souls in order to feed her own emptiness.

Truly, she is a fearsome adversary, but the princess is unafraid. She has already vanquished her own demon in the Forest of Forgetting and she is ready for whatever fate may await her.

Steeling her heart and taking up her reins, the princess prepares to...

Get out of the car.

Stretch my body.

Lock the door.

As the warmth drains out of me, I stand for a long moment in the frigid air and watch two glossy black crows land just a few short metres away.

They regard me with tilted heads and curious eyes.

Odin's birds.

Dark omens of bad things yet to come.

They fluff their ebony feathers against the cold and caw and call, strut and peck. They bounce along the uneven blacktop for a few quick strides and then, powerfully beating their densely feathered wings, rise up into the sky with a fluid grace. I track their flight path from right to left, watching as they cross the golden disc of the sun, made small with distance, and disappear from view behind an ugly tower block of flats. I'm no haruspex, but, as portents go, I can think of better.

As the day begins to peek above the railway track, a train passes, thunderously loud even over the roar of the busy road. The locomotive shuttles the packed tin can commuters onwards, like a high-speed Charon ferrying souls across the river Styx.

Did any of the train sardines get the career they wanted?

Does anyone remember who they once thought they were going to be?

…at last the trees begin to thin and sunlight streams through the previously dense foliage in shafts. The Forest of Forgetting thins into the Wood of Accepted Banality and, eventually, gives way to a vast open plain and a village of tiny huts.

Then the princess finally sees it, standing black and bleak and impenetrable high up on a hill straight ahead; the Castle of Play The Game Or Get Fired.

The princess takes a long, deep and steadying breath. She knows that soon she must face the abhorrent she-devil that she has sought. The bold pony tosses her long mane impatiently and paws the ground with one strong foreleg. Valiant as ever, the stout mare is ready to go, eager to meet the next challenge head-on.

Together the princess and the pony stand a moment longer in…

The early sun's first gentle glow.

I drink it in as though I will never see it again.

This time of year, when the days are short and the nights are long, it seems as though that might, in fact, be true.

I stand in the desolate carpark as though I'm waiting for a miracle to happen.

It's strewn with rubbish here and there; discarded plastic carrier bags like deflated balloons and empty take-away containers devoid of almost everything save a few scraps left behind for scavenging foxes. There are cigarette butts, spent Lotto tickets and scratch-cards, crumpled and bloated from rain. The ground is littered with the detritus of the working class; Friday night treats and Saturday night hopes both equally abandoned in this forsaken place.

At least here I can still be me.

I can think thoughts that have nothing to do with customer service, databases and KPIs.

Along the perimeter of the lot there's a patch of scrubby grass and a sepia-toned wall that's overgrown with brittle brown blackberry bushes and verdant ivy, which crawls across the pitted bricks and settles into even the shallowest of cracks, like a mountaineer clinging desperately to an escarpment, searching for a secure place to hold. Beneath the shade of the snarled overgrowth all smaller plants have been strangled out of existence.

Somewhere in there is a clumsy metaphor for life; the suffocating of Average Joe and Plain Jane by the pernicious greed of those above them, who in their own turn are each scrambling over one another in a frantic effort to find their place in the sun.

But who wants to sound like just another whingeing millennial cliché?

...and the princess and the pony advance towards the final battle.

Unafraid, they cross the vast, featureless tundra towards the cluster of crude houses. The Empty Village of My Heart skulks at the foot of the terrible queen's evil lair. The streets are deserted. Overturned carts and abandoned wagons speak of hasty evacuation. A forgotten ball and a cast-away rag-doll indicate the speed with which the panicked citizens fled.

Lifeless and abandoned, nothing stirs before them until, suddenly, a large and powerful...

Black Cat appears.

I see him every day.

I don't know what his true name might be, but that's who he'll always be to me.

Black Cat.

As a monicker it's not very creative, but it describes him perfectly.

The hunter prowls along the edge of the pavement his paws making no sound at all as they lift and fall. His stealthy passage hugs close against a garden fence. With the skill of experience, he stalks some unseen, mousey prey.

I follow him for a while, as our paths run together. He seems either not to notice or not to mind and carries on about his business until, sadly, we part ways. I turn into the dilapidated swing park that acts as a cut-through to the office and he continues stalking his quarry.

The playground is bordered on either side by high shrubs that are still thick with ever-green leaves. Starlings shift nervously between the branches, hopping from twig to twig in a neurotic dance, their speckled breasts and iridescent feathers shimmering. Some of them sing their songs out loud, bravely proclaiming the arrival of the new day. Others stretch their wings and prepare to take to the air as I pass.

A damp mist has formed in the enclosed space where an abandoned slide and a forgotten roundabout crouch beside a matched pair of battered swings that were once a vibrant fire-engine red. Light falls from the street lamps illuminating the path, spreading like an angel's wings on either side of the lamppost, catching the drops of moisture that hang in the thick air so that they glisten and gleam.

The sound of my sensible, hard-soled shoes striking the cracked cement of the path is muffled by the fog. It swallows up even the roar of the traffic, turning it into nothing more than a muted drone. The bushes rustle and some of the birds make good on their promise and do at last take flight, startled off of their perches and into the peculiar half-light.

One of the empty swings groans pitifully on its rusted hinges, crying out for oil or grease.

There is a deep sadness about this place, a mournful air of rejection. Children must have played here once, but I've not seen a single one, not in the ten years that I've been working this job, come to slide or spin or swing. It's as though all the joy has been sucked out of this barren place, leached out of the very air, just as the colour has drained from the once bright paint.

In a few more steps the moist vapour begins to clear. As I leave the secluded park behind, the office looms black and stark before me in all its plate-glass-fronted glory, like some hulking brute preparing to swallow me whole with one great bite of its fetid maw.

164

And like a sacrificial lamb to the slaughter I tap my ID card against the secure entry system and walk slowly into the sterile lobby, lifeless apart from one dying potted plant.

...the narrow dirt streets ahead are entirely empty, devoid of all life. Not even a stray dog walks abroad. Doors hang broken from their coarse wooden frames and the place has a look of death about it, like a gutted fish lying stinking on the riverbank.

The Empty Village of My Heart is a barren place, nothing at all like the lively hamlet that the princess remembers from her youth.

Suddenly on her toes, the pony starts and shies at some movement deep within the shadows. The princess saws on the reins and holds the prancing mare steady. For the briefest moment the princess thinks she sees a small child crouching beside a ruined house, but then the apparition begins to wail in a voice that no human throat could utter and other voices, from all around, join in the doleful keen.

Without delay, the princess sets her heels to the pony's sides, so that they gallop the rest of the way through that haunted place toward the dread fort's gates, leaving behind the spectres screaming in the shade. Together they race up steps carved from grey-black rock, rough-hewn and steep. The pony's hooves ring out loud and drown the pitiful cries coming from the phantoms down below.

The pony skitters to a halt before a wall of seemingly impenetrable stone, tail held high, breath coming hard and fast. When the princess manages to calm her mount long enough to take a look, she sees that the portcullis is up and the way ahead suspiciously unguarded.

The princess senses that she is surely walking into a trap and yet she presses on. She and the pony walk quickly beneath the murder holes as they pass through the gate, neither one of them desiring to linger in that treacherous place.

Onwards, into the fire-blackened courtyard they rush, where they come face-to-face with...

My boss.

She appears before I'm ready, darting out of her office like a funnel-web springing from its trap.

She really is the stuff of nightmares, with her neatly cropped black bob and heavily kohl rimmed eyes; a phantasm in a poorly fitting suit. She's whippet thin and dresses all in black like a villain from a pantomime. Her nails are long and scarlet, her narrow lips painted the same shade. She wears tall stiletto high-heels and teeters about in them as though she's proving something by making herself uncomfortable.

Really she could almost be comical, if she wasn't the underqualified thief of my autonomy.

"Good morning," she says brightly, a note in her voice close to hysteria.

I grunt something noncommittal in response.

"When you've made yourself a cuppa, come on into my office." She smiles widely with suspiciously white teeth - a disconcertingly reptilian expression. And her eyes, her eyes bulge dangerously beneath overplucked, tadpole brows. I can't decide whether she's happy or hungry. "We need to have a quick chat."

And there it is.

That most sickening of workplace phrases.

The death knell of every career.

The Chat.

...and up to the top of the highest tower, following a narrow, spiral staircase, the princess makes her ascent, having left her noble steed waiting patiently below. Her legs burn as she climbs and with every step the atmosphere becomes more and more oppressive. The princess can feel the hag's malice reaching for her, rolling down the twisting stair.

Dark magik.

Wicked enchantments are being cast.

The princess makes the sign of the cross and prays.

"Lord, watch over me and keep me safe."

And then there she is, filling the doorway ahead with her presence.

The nightmare fiend grins maniacally, her feverish, half-crazed eyes stretched wide. She is dressed like the night, in flowing black robes. Pale skin stretches across her skull-like face and her taloned fingers claw at the empty air. The demon-queen beckons the princess close and, as the heroine steps boldly into the forbidden chamber, with enchantments she slams the door tightly shut behind her.

A low rumble fills the air and beyond the castle walls a mighty storm begins to brew. Lightning flashes and the clouds growl. Rain lashes down in sheets, and turns to hail. Hailstones the size of fists, whipped by the wind, bash and batter the keep with a din like the very halls of Pandemonium. The pressure inside the room builds, as the tempest now rages inside the tower itself, summoned by the sorceress's might.

Now the princess knows for certain that there is but one way she might escape.

Here in the Castle of Career Suicide there are no second chances, so she does the only thing that she reasonably can. With a deep breath and a combative glare the princess raises her vorpal sword aloft and in defiant challenge shouts...

"Fuck you?" My boss's lizard-lipped mouth falls open in appalled disbelief.

Slack-jawed she gapes as I turn triumphantly on my heel and jerk open the door to her office. I stand for a moment in dramatic pause before banging it loudly shut once more, so hard that the plexiglass cubicle shakes.

In the corridor I walk with my head held high, advancing in triumphal procession back the way I came. I pass colleagues shuffling dismally inside to begin their dreary days and, in spite of myself, I'm smiling now, like a grimace.

Before Alice got to Wonderland, she fell down a deep, dark hole.

Is this a beginning in the end?

Is it time to stop?

Not until I stand once more outside in the glacial wintery chill do I dare to take a breath, sucking down air as though I had drowned.

A large white seagull ghosts by on silent wings, calling mournfully, an incongruous visitor to this fume-choked city, just passing through from sunny shores far, far away. He sings of lost sailors and long voyages taken at sea. He cries the sound of waves breaking and tells of surf washing the sand in quiet hidden coves. And like a spirit he passes by, soon lost in the eldritch fog that still hangs damply over the decrepit play park.

I'm cold in my bones, but the sun is starting to rise higher. Soon its warmth will burn off the frost and the last of the haze.

I touch my cheek gingerly with one probing fingertip and find that the grimace is transformed into an unfamiliar beam. Underused muscles ache. My expression has become one of pure, unadulterated joy, so uncharacteristic that I can't remember the last time my face moved this way.

Black Cat reappears from beneath one of the dripping bushes with something small and fluffy hanging limply from his mouth. I look directly into the narrow slits of his dragon-yellow eyes and he blinks slowly at me once, before disappearing back into the shrubbery.

We're all mad here.

...then outside in the glorious sunshine the victorious princess stood, the last vestiges of the fallen enemy's squall quickly dying away.

With far-sight she stares out through the open gateway and watches as the ragged clouds lift to reveal a New World of Possibility and the graceful arc of a rainbow stretches wide across the horizon.

The princess hearkens to the sounds of life returning to the Empty Village of My Heart beyond the castle's walls and knows that the place won't be empty for long. With the evil witch's spell broken, the tethered souls trapped there will finally be able to move on and so the land will become beautiful and bountiful once again.

Her day's work done and the undoable deed undertaken, the princess climbs up into her creaking leather saddle and leans forward to caress the pony's soft, snowy neck. She entwines her fingers in the damp fur and kisses her courageous friend gratefully. The princess knows that she could never have achieved so much without her. She gives the pony's sides a gentle squeeze and the mare's hard hooves ring out a carillon against the stone.

Onward bound the princess and the pony go, together towards a future unknown, two flightless birds free once more to live and love and roam.

The End.

Dead Wood

Emily Chapman

I am paid to be a liar, and I excel at it.

I write the articles in the papers. There aren't many people who can do that. Not convincingly. People are too wary of believing what they read now.

I took the first fee they offered me, and so they hired me on the spot. There are probably better writers out there, but they want more pay, so I guess we'll never know. I'm not fussy, and at that time I hadn't eaten in three days.

With the job you get a flat. I have a room with a bathroom and kitchen attached. A desk. They threw that in like a last-minute thought. A wage. Every day I get up, I check the machine that prints things anytime they want me. I write what they want me to write, I turn it in.

Nat drops by now and again. He works in the Information Centre. With the books that no one reads anymore – that no one *can* read anymore. He doesn't speak about it much, not unless you can get a drink or two down him.

He was sat on the bed last night, on his second drink, and began quoting bits of the books. I hadn't realised he looked at them closely enough to remember substantial bits of them. He never used to be able to do that. I stop typing, spin on my chair, and watch him. He's quoting 'Ozymandias'.

Someone walks past the door to my flat, the floorboards creak. Nat stops abruptly.

'Sorry.'

'It's okay.'

'No, I really am -'

'I said, it's okay. Don't worry about it'

I start typing again, and after a while Nat leaves.

He struggles more than I do. At times I can make myself forget about the things we used to read. Nat can't. That's why he works in the Information Centre, with the books and the dust.

*

At first, we thought it was a supply and demand thing. But then bookstores were closing. Then it became impossible to get anything fiction. Just non-fiction stuff. Anything that was a distraction was gone. Things changed when Nat and I were about eighteen. Gradually at first. Books from writers outside, in translation, became harder to come by. Then, age limits became a thing - which was a problem when it came to reading lists for universities. As the machines started breaking down and we needed more people to fix them, or we ran out of drugs and didn't have enough scientists or raw materials to make them, books that were fantasy or fiction became harder to come by.

It isn't exactly illegal to read the stuff you already have, but you're encouraged to get rid of it. To be an active member of society instead.

Anything that you have to read is short and to the point. Like the papers I write. I used to write different stuff. For fun. Poems and things. I have notebooks under the bed. I keep them. I worry that I've kept them, but I can't get rid of them.

Some people kicked up a fuss at first. Those who could afford it left, the ones who made a living from writing the more popular books. Moved abroad. Those who couldn't afford it, buttoned it. The money that used to go into the arts was relocated to keep things going. Chugging along.

The only ones who read things other than the government papers are people like Nat. All the books the government could round up are down there in his department, safe from being read. The ones with the highest age limits. Nat is supposed to read and research and report back – help out with the displays. Sometimes the books are put out in glass cases with notes next to them on why we don't read them anymore, pinned there like dead butterflies.

*

Nat's having a hard time recently. It was the anniversary of Toby's death yesterday, so Nat came around here and had a few drinks. Nat drinks for both of us.

Toby was Nat's partner. A painter.

He accepted an offer to have his work displayed in a gallery when we were about twenty. It had been up a couple of weeks, then it disappeared. The gallery had introduced an exhibition on "Important Political Figures" instead.

When he asked about his work, they told him it was no longer suitable for the gallery. When he asked for it back, the manager said they couldn't give him it back.

He understood then.

I'd seen Toby the day before it happened. He'd been here. Had a drink, then headed home to Nat.

Nat rang an hour later to see if I had heard from Toby.

We found him in the street a few yards from home.

*

Nat practically lives here now. Sleeps on the sofa. He doesn't want to go back to an empty house anymore.

He leaves for work at 8am and comes home at 5pm. Then sits and watches reality TV. Eats. Sleeps.

He hasn't mentioned the books in a long time.

*

I leave Nat to look after himself for a couple of hours while I go to the shops for some food.

When I come back, he's holding one of my notebooks. He jumps as the door closes.

I put the chain on.

'I didn't realise you'd kept these.'

'I didn't plan on telling you I had.'

He has the grace to look ashamed.

'I spilled my coffee and when I was wiping it up -'

'- and you thought you'd have a nosy under the bed.'

'No, I -'

'It wasn't a question.'

We're both silent.

'I couldn't get rid of them.'

'You shouldn't have to.'

*

Nat is late home. Only by an hour or so.

I don't know where he's gone. Maybe to see Toby. Toby's headstone, I should say.

I take my notebooks out.

I used to write all the time. I filled so many notebooks. Most of them had blotches of ink and smudges on the pages. Some were water-damaged.

The underside of my left pinkie finger was constantly stained blue back then.

I want to write. But it gets harder and harder. Anything done purely for vanity reasons is dead wood. We have too much else to think about. Like feeding ourselves.

I snap the notebook shut and stuff it back under the bed.

*

When I get up Nat's phone is ringing. It's a number without a name to it.

His background is still Toby. Holding a paintbrush, with red acrylic blooming like poppies on his T-shirt.

*

One of my notebooks is missing.

Nat is late home again.

Three days in a row, that is.

*

They're running the Night Press. They never do that.

They're sending through the information in fifteen minutes.

*

It's my poems.

They don't know it's my poems. But they've sent me my poems, and I know it's them.

*

I kick Nat out. He comes home to find me with the print-out, trying to write up a call for people to come forward and dob me in if they had any information.

He's given the notebook to someone he met at work. A "friend" he says. Someone who needed poems.

178

'Needed them for what? *To read in bed?* How *dense* can you be, Nat?'

'I didn't -'

'They were probably undercover!'

'They don't know it's yours!'

'Oh, *even* better!'

'Look, there's a group who want to -'

'Oh, great. *Great.*'

'But – you'll never believe who -'

'I want you to leave.'

'It'll be completely underground. *There are people working in government jobs there!* Anyone who wants to join us enough will -'

'I want you to leave.'

'What? Where -'

'I want you to pack your bag and *leave.*'

Nat packs his bag. He only has one. I assume he's gone back to his place.

I feel bad, but I can't – he can't – think this is okay.

I can't finish this paper on catching myself with him here. It's due in one hour.

*

I haven't seen Nat in a week.

179

I rang him yesterday.

He didn't say much over the phone.

He'd seen the paper, he's apologised again.

He's coming over later.

*

Nat's not turned up yet.

I bought him some soup to make up for kicking him out.

I hope he has my notebook and didn't give the whole thing away.

*

Nat should have been here an hour ago.

I might ring him. Sometimes he just loses track of time -

A print-out just came through. I'll check it while I wait.

*

They sent over a photo of him for the article. Doctored.

It's him and Toby. Toby is holding a champagne flute instead of his paint brush.

It's from his first exhibition. His arm is around Nat.

The banner that had his name and title of the collection he'd painted is doctored too.

It says something about a "Young Business Owner Award".

It was from his first exhibition.

They want to run a story on the tragic death of a couple, just a few years apart. Toby aged 20, Nat aged 23.

Both killed in separate, unconnected hit and runs, just minutes from their home.

The Boss says he knows I knew Nat. He's attached his condolences at the end of the message.

*

Nat made some origami cranes when he was last over.

From the old print-outs that had come through.

They're all sat on my desk.

When I finish typing the paper and send it off, I sit and stare at them a long time.

I'm going over to his place tomorrow.

He has a cat that usually looks after itself, but I'd best bring her back here.

*

I've got the cat. And my notebook.

Nat's place is a mess. I don't remember him even having been that messy. He used to slide a coaster under my drink if I put it on a bare table.

I was relieved to see that notebook.

He'd hidden it behind a loose panel of wood in the back of his kitchen cupboard. He used to pull the same trick in our student house. He'd hide weed there. Back when the three of us and another girl shared a flat together.

I hide my notebook under my bed with the others.

*

I've had some more information on Nat.

People have bought the idea that he was a small business owner. "Home Grown" is the phrasing we use.

They're interested in the story.

Even now, people like tragedy.

The Boss sent over another note.

The officer working on the case needs interviewing. He's asked if I want to do it and attached contact details. I never interview people.

Maybe he thinks he's doing me a favour.

*

I meet Amy in a coffee shop.

She hasn't changed. She hugs me and I pat her back awkwardly.

'This is all a bit odd, I know.'

She's in civilian clothes. Not the up-to-date uniform of officers. They carry arms all the time now.

I had always wondered what happened to Amy. She'd had her eye on a Law Enforcement position years ago, did a few stints with them, just shadowing.

Safer than doing art or literature, it turns out.

She lived with Nat, Toby and I. Four-bedroom house, see.

We were friends at one point, but I guess we just grew apart once she made the move into her current career. I haven't heard from her in a couple of years.

'Yeah, I'm glad it's you though.' I'm lying through my teeth. I'd rather it was anyone else.

She smiles. 'Yeah, same. I wasn't when I saw him. But – I wouldn't have wanted someone else to go with him to the hospital.'

'Hospital?'

'He wasn't dead when we got there, he was just hanging in there. Dead by the time we got to the hospital. The paramedics tried.'

The part of me that must write this, the part ignoring that it's Nat who's dead, thinks that'll be interesting. Not dead when they got there. A few minutes from help when he gave in.

'Did he say anything about the car that hit him?'

'No. Forensics think it hit him from behind. The impact broke most of his ribs and fractured his skull.'

She says it so matter-of-factly.

I down my coffee, which is still hot, and croak *thanks* before I get up. Someone else can interview her.

'Wait, don't you want to catch up properly sometime? Come over to mine?'

I can't think of an excuse right now, so I nod and promise I'll text her.

When I get in, the packaging from the soup is still in the bin. I take the trash out. Then I stand in the shower for a long time.

*

Amy messaged me. I didn't expect her to really want to catch up.

Amy had always had a nose for when people aren't doing what they're meant to. Which Nat wasn't.

What's more, she acts on it. It's kind of her job.

Like mine is to write papers, and not do anything wrong.

She can't come around here. But if I tell her where to go, that looks suspicious. I don't know if she knows what Nat was up to.

I offer to go to hers.

Nat's cat is doing my head in.

She yowls at the fax machine a lot.

It's a nice apartment, so she has nothing to complain about. It's light and airy. Windows and stuff. I brought her litter tray over, but she's ignoring it. I've cleaned up more cat pee than anything else this week.

*

Amy only lives thirty minutes walk away. I didn't realise she was so close.

It's odd none of us ran into her before now.

It's a swanky apartment. All glass and metal. She's on the 30th floor.

She answers the door in jeans and a T-shirt. Holding two drinks.

'Oh, I don't drink anymore Amy – can I just get a water or something?'

'Sure! Sparkling water okay? I have lemon for it.'

'That'd be great.'

I have no idea where to put my jacket. Everything is white and cream.

Standard government employee housing. Mine's like this, but a bit shabbier. It's different when it's someone else's place though.

Here, everything smells like magnolias.

We sit down.

We talk a while, about Nat.

She asks me what I'm working on at the moment, other than Nat's story.

I tell her it's just the standard front-page stuff. She seems impressed, a little surprised.

'I didn't expect you to go in for that kind of stuff! But, well, good for you!'

I'm not sure what she means by this.

'You just seemed like such a – not someone who wanted to be told what to write.' She's looking at me very intently. 'We all know you were a writer.'

I don't say anything. I take a drink and the bubbles feel like they're corroding my tongue.

'Well,' she continues, 'I mean… didn't you want to be published? You did get some stuff published?'

'Um, no, Amy, I didn't.'

'Oh,' she laughs, 'it must have been someone else I was thinking of!'

I can taste metal. I force a laugh too. 'Well, weren't we all writers at some point?'

She doesn't like being reminded that she started out on a literature degree, before a law conversion and then going into law enforcement. Writing, books, poems - all dirty words to her now.

I feel the friction crackle in the air and realise I've just outstayed my welcome. She laughs again.

'Yeah, I suppose we were! Not all of us carried around those notebooks though.'

She's trained to do this. I remind myself. *If you lie, she'll know.*

'I did used to love my notebooks,' I say vaguely.

She's not sure what to do with that. I take advantage of this:

'Well, I'd best be getting back to let the cat out!'

'Oh, I didn't know you had a cat,' she says as she jumps up to get my coat.

'Well, she was Nat's. I've kind of adopted her.'

'That's sweet, although I didn't realise you were still so close to Nat?'

'What do you mean?' I ask, putting my coat on. It's an old coat. I've had it for years.

'Well, I figured it was just some horrible coincidence that you had to write the article. Seems a little morbid that they'd give it to you.'

'Who else would they give it to?'

'I don't know. Someone a little less attached, maybe.'

She looks at me standing in my coat with my hand on the door, head cocked to one side, smiling sweetly.

'You look exactly the same as you did back then, you know? No matter what, some people barely change.'

She reaches forwards and opens the door herself as my arm swings down to my side.

'I'll see you soon.'

If I have anything to say about it, I will never see Amy again.

*

I have all my notebooks on the bed. The cat is sat watching me.

I'm holding one. The one Nat had.

I've just pulled something from the pocket at the back.

187

It's an address and number in Nat's writing.

Under it he's scrawled: *"My name is Ozymandias, King of Kings; Look on my Works, ye Mighty, and despair! Nothing beside remains. Round the decay of that colossal Wreck, boundless and bare the lone and level sands stretch far away."*

*

The address is a café on the edge of town.

Quiet.

The owner doesn't seem bothered by me.

I've brought a paper. I order coffee and watch.

I've nearly finished when he walks in.

I recognise him from the Information Centre. He's the one who pins the books and the plaques Nat writes into the display cases. He's clocked me. There's a mutual understanding that we are here for each other.

He gets a coffee and sits. No introductions, just:

'You're Nat's friend?'

Most people don't have the time for small talk anymore.

He's seen me before, in the Information Centre. Seen me walking around looking for Nat or some records for something I'm meant to be writing about.

'I was sorry to hear about him.'

'You should be.'

'I told him to be careful. He wasn't subtle enough.'

'So it *was* about this writing thing? Listen, this isn't - wasn't - his fault. If you just let things be -'

'Let this carry on? Let them take away more books?' He's saying it quietly, but for a minute I stop breathing.

He's old, a year or two older than me, I reckon. Mid-twenties.

He was probably there. A lot of people were there.

*

For a little while after people started noticing books were going missing, that spoken word nights, libraries and art galleries were being closed, some of us had tried to go underground.

Nat had never given up on the idea, even after Toby. *Especially* after Toby.

We'd found an old warehouse. Nat, Toby, myself and some others.

People came from all over. Brought poems and stories and songs. Drinks.

About an hour in, they arrived.

Either we were too loud, or someone ratted us out, or we got followed. They caught about half of the people at the event.

None of what we were doing was technically illegal at the time. This was about a month before they really cracked down. Maybe it was why they really cracked down – a bunch of twenty-somethings drinking and singing in a warehouse.

They arrested people on the grounds of being in a derelict building and being drunk and disorderly.

I got the job with the paper two weeks later, lied and said I'd read about the busted warehouse thing in the paper, but hadn't known anyone there.

Toby, Nat and I had got out in the confusion.

The people who came in, swarming around like fat black flies in their bulky uniforms, armed to the teeth, had headed for the band on the stage first. You could hear what was happening over the speakers.

When I got the job, I waited for a print-out about what had happened following the arrests. Nothing ever came through. It was like it had never happened.

I hid my notebooks and tried to forget about it. I had a few slip-ups at first. Read and wrote a few things for myself.

Toby carried on painting regardless.

After Toby I stopped writing altogether.

Nat started drinking.

*

His name is Ryan. He says he'd been working in a bookshop when it all happened. When that place closed, he fell back on his education and now teaches physics.

'Who suspects a physics teacher of dabbling in the arts?' he asks wryly.

He says that he'd been at the gig, but we'd not met. There had been a lot of people there.

'I *knew* Nat didn't write that stuff!'

'He told you he wrote it?' I don't know if I'm grateful or angry.

'Yeah, swore blind. I knew it though. I *knew* it. He wasn't much of a poet. I listened to him for his stories. That chick knew it wasn't his too – blonde hair. Annie? Anna?'

'Amy?'

'That's it! Yeah, she knew. Nat messaged me, said he'd met an old friend by chance, got talking, and she wanted to come along. I wasn't too happy that he'd been *that* quick to speak, but – she seemed nice. Keen. Said he'd known her a long time.'

Toby and I had held Amy at arm's length towards the end of knowing her. Toby didn't trust her at all. I tended to err on the side of caution but was friendly enough. Nat though, few people were as friendly as him. It was like living with those books had addled his brain.

'You said – Amy knew it was mine?'

'She said it was familiar,' Ryan shrugs.

When we lived together, Toby and I would sit in the living room whilst I read pieces out to get the tempo right. To check myself when I got things wrong.

Amy would stop and lean on the doorframe sometimes, clap at the end.

'Has Amy been in touch recently?'

'Nah, I guess she's been spooked.'

*

The cat is quiet as I put the key into the lock. Usually she yowls and scratches the door. Especially when it rains.

I flick the lights on and call her. Nat named her Mavis. Stupid name for a cat.

She doesn't appear.

I walk into my room.

The bedcovers have been pulled off. The cupboards torn open and the contents thrown onto the floor. The windows, all four, are open. I go into the bathroom.

The cabinet above the sink is empty, bottles and jars rolling around on the floor.

I kneel by the toilet and heave.

When I'm done, I dislodge the tile by the pipe that comes out of the toilet. Behind it are the three notebooks I keep. I took a leaf from Nat's book and hid them there. I replace the tile.

I pick up the phone and ring Amy.

'Amy, someone had been into my apartment.'

'Oh! God, no, stay on the phone, I'll be right over'

I grind my teeth waiting for her to arrive.

When she does, in full uniform, including arms, she picks her way over the debris gingerly.

I suddenly think better of this. We aren't squabbling over a gas bill now.

It's been raining, and with the open windows, everything is wet.

'I'm – who would – I'm so sorry. The door wasn't forced?'

'The door was fine. The cat's missing though.'

'They came through the window?'

I nod. 'That's what it looks like.'

'Do you think they were looking for something?' She hasn't looked me in the face yet, but now she does.

'What on earth would they be looking for?'

'Well, I don't -'

'Wait, Amy. What if -'

'Yes?'

I swallow. 'What if they were looking for information, the stuff that I'm sent to write the articles for the papers?'

I see her jaw twitch. 'I'm not sure…' - she manages to catch herself - 'I suppose that's one thing.'

'What else could it be?' I shrug.

We're both silent for a while.

'It must be that,' she sighs. 'I can get someone over to dust for prints?'

She doesn't seem too bothered.

I walk to the open window and slam it closed.

'No. It's okay. Nothing's missing, I've looked. I'd rather just tidy up and lock all of the doors and windows.'

I stare at her long and hard. She knows.

She nods and turns. 'Make sure you do lock them all. God knows what people are up to out there.'

She heads for the open door. I don't follow.

'Oh! Amy, there is one thing!'

She spins around.

'Can you ask Law Enforcement to keep an eye out for my cat? Answers to Mavis.'

Her jaw tenses again. She struggles for a moment, then nods tersely. The door slams behind her.

I shouldn't have done that. I didn't need to.

Some things are better left unsaid.

But it made me feel better.

I sit on the bed and breathe for a few minutes, think about what to do next.

*

The next few days pass without much incidence.

Print-outs come through. I write the articles. I don't hear from Ryan.

He was either lying low, or didn't want to speak to me, or -

It doesn't bear thinking about.

Maybe it's a good thing I haven't heard. Nat trusted him, and -

A message falls into my inbox.

It's Ryan.

He wants me to come to the next meeting. These underground artists, living like moles.

We're one down now, he says.

I recline in my desk chair, looking at the stack of articles.

I can't go.

I want to.

Is it really that important?

Yes.

I should just forget about it. Who needs poems?

You do.

*

They meet in Ryan's flat. Not a government building. On the edge of the city, close to suburbia.

I have no idea how Ryan, who works in the Information Centre, has managed to hang onto this flat. Usually they like to put you up in a government flat when you work for the government. Whether you're a cleaner or a politician.

It's an old house, split into four flats. Ryan's is on the top floor.

In the room there are five of us. Ryan, myself, two other girls, and one other guy. They all know each other. All knew Nat.

One of them works with Ryan in the Information Centre. The other two do menial work. Washing pots and scrubbing floors. The stuff I did before I took the paper job.

I still wince at the smell of bleach.

Someone asks where Amy is. Ryan doesn't say anything. He looks at me.

'Oh,' the girl murmurs.

He's letting them believe Amy is gone too. The same way as Nat. Or has been scared off. Something like that.

I suppose it's better not to panic them by letting them know she's a rat.

Ryan tells me later that Amy doesn't know where he lives; they'd met in Nat's house the time she came to the group.

People have brought small sketchbooks. Notebooks with scrawls on every page. One of the girls has written across the page, then turned it 180 degrees, and written across it again. Paper is expensive.

I haven't brought my notebook. I don't know if I want to bring anything yet.

Ryan introduces me as Nat's ghost writer. I smile weakly. It's more of a grimace. There are some approving nods around the room.

It's almost sad. These people meeting here just to share some poems and ask whether their picture needed more cerulean or more Prussian blue?

I kind of like it.

Despite how sad it is.

We spend two hours talking, playing music to mask the conversation from the flat below.

As we're packing up to leave, one of the girls asks if I can bring some of my poems. If they can use them.

'For what?'

'Oh, we take bits of poems and distribute them. Leave them in bus stations and stuff.'

'Why?' Though I know, I think, the answer.

'If we don't do it, who will? The more people who see them and start to write, the easier it'll be to – to change things.'

'Isn't that a bit… isn't it asking for trouble?'

She shrugs. 'Yeah, but if you gotta write, you gotta write.'

*

The group meets sporadically.

It's always a text from Ryan, which I must delete immediately afterwards.

It's never predictable, but I expect the texts now. I wait for them.

Nat and Toby are gone, Amy is (thankfully) taking the hint and staying away.

I went and looked for Mavis. She hasn't come back.

When animals get out, well -

Supermarkets have limited stock now. If you run out of tokens, if you're desperate… it's understandable.

Without all of them, what else do I have to do?

*

The machine is spitting out requests more and more frequently. Almost frantically.

I write the article. I make up lies. I send it off. I get paid.

One morning, early, something new comes through.

The Boss wants me to write something... different.

He notices, he says, that on my application I've listed a now defunct degree.

He figures, he says, I can help with a new project. They'll pay me well.

The government wants to introduce a new brand of *poetry*.

I read that word again.

Poetry?

Government approved poetry?

It'll certainly be a good ruse. Writing for the government to cover up the illegal writing I'm doing outside of work.

I agree. I agree even more when I get my first pay cheque. Nearly double.

I suppose they've driven all the other writers into hiding.

*

I explain this at the next meeting.

They're all silent. I see the group physically cracking down the centre with regards to this.

Ryan is quiet for a while, then he changes the subject.

*

The poems they want aren't really poems.

They're very... very much a call to band together and "make the country great again".

I hate writing them, but it's easy cash.

I tell The Boss I don't want my name on them.

*

At the same time as this, I have taken the group up on the offer to distribute proper poetry.

This means anything not focused on the motherland.

Sometimes on the weather. Sometimes on revolution. Sometimes on sex. Sometimes on war.

Sometimes on politicians we don't much like.

I get more daring with this.

One day, I accidentally drop a small, folded sheet. A draft.

A man behind me shouts: "Hey, miss! You dropped this!"

He hands it back to me, saying that if it's a receipt, I'll need it. Things aren't made like they used to be.

*

I start getting print-outs through about the poems we're leaving around the city.

The essays and pamphlets one of the others made too.

I enjoy typing up these papers, laughing the whole time.

*

Ryan messages me with the date and time of the next group. It's this evening.

I pack my notebooks, walk over and head up to the flat.

The music is playing, and I can hear someone talking – one of the girls.

Good, I hate being the first one to arrive. I knock and let myself in.

In the living room is a woman with a sweep of blonde hair.

I hear a bolt slide across the door, then feel a hand on my shoulder.

Ryan motions towards a chair.

Neither of them speaks for a while. They just watch me.

I watch back.

Amy clears her throat and faces Ryan.

'I think we should take her fingers. That'd solve the problem.'

Ryan had told me to keep my hands on the arms of the chair with my palms facing down, but now I ball my hands into fists.

Ryan smiles. It's a horrible, horrible smile.

'That's not our call, Amy.'

She always had been a fucking vigilante.

'Nat -'

'Don't start.'

'I wasn't going to'

'Hm.'

Screw it.

'You made him think you were his friend.'

'You made the same mistake.'

'You really think I've been friendly recent-'

I feel my chest cave in. She doesn't mean now.

It was my fault.

I think Amy sees my face change. She smiles a little wider.

I'd spoken to Amy a week before the gig.

Invited her along.

She wasn't a fully-fledged officer, just doing a placement in the Law Enforcement Office. She was working all the hours available, had her eye on being one of the big guns. She still hung around us. I figured she needed a break. That she was distant because she was stressed.

It was only afterwards, when she cut ties, when she quickly moved up through the ranks –

I feel the twenty-year-old me crumple inside the twenty-three-year-old shell.

Amy hadn't turned up that night – but Law Enforcement had. Swept away forty plus people, off the face of the earth.

'What happened to them?'

Amy smiles, and doesn't say anything.

*

We sit like that for half an hour. An hour.

Ryan has the courtesy to fill me in.

Nat had shared the poems I'd written with him and the group.

Ryan had told Nat about the group, whispered about it to him over the banned books in the bowels of the Information Centre. It hadn't taken long to persuade him.

Amy was convinced that Nat and I still had something going on. She'd put Ryan onto it. He's a mole stationed in the Information Centre. It attracts unsavoury characters, he says. He just spots them, then works on them.

The other members of the group have no idea that this is some kind of papery honeytrap, and I gather I won't be the one telling them.

Nat had "run into" Amy, and she'd wheedled her way in. Though of course, she was already in.

Nat checked he could bring Amy with Ryan, who said she was more than welcome – after some appropriate grumbling.

They must have been laughing at Nat so hard behind his back.

'For all the books he read, he wasn't the smartest, was he?'

Ryan and Amy are both Law Enforcement. They "met for the first time" in Nat's house.

Once Ryan told him about the group, Nat had volunteered his house as their meeting place.

'He really didn't like being alone, did he?' Ryan hisses.

My throat is contracting.

The one truth Ryan had told me was that he had been at the gig a few years ago. Junior Law Enforcement.

I stop listening then.

*

They'll be here soon, whoever Ryan just called on his phone.

Amy has decided they have time to kill.

She goes into my bag and pulls out a notebook, then she pulls a lighter from her jacket.

'Don't -'

She slaps me - harder than I thought she'd be able to. The room shatters, then comes fizzing back into view.

When my eyes focus, she's ripping a page out. She's holding it to the flame.

After that, Ryan tears the pages out, and Amy sets them alight.

They curl up and turn black, one by one. I watch the still smoking pages at my feet, the words ash, dissolving into the carpet.

Ryan tosses the gutted cover to my feet.

Without looking away, without stopping smiling, Amy goes back into the bag.

Then they start on the next one.

By The Book

Jane Carnaffan

"But Edith is the company, my dear. Sue the company for an unfair contract and you're suing her. You signed a deal with the devil herself. You know she won't budge an inch. And unfair isn't unlawful."

Aggie looked down at her hands, and examined her fingers fiercely in an attempt to control her anger. The ring finger of her left hand was bare. For over a decade she hadn't had time for any kind of relationship other than with her work. And Edith. It was these hands, these fingers, that had written twelve novels for Edith Mulgrave, literary agent, editor and publisher extraordinaire. She had one more to write before she could be released from her crippling contract.

"Believe me. I've seen too many promising young writers fall into this trap."

Well, you would've, wouldn't you? Aggie thought. Since you're Edith's lawyer and you draw up the damned things!

"Edith has this gift, you see, for spotting new talent, for nurturing and moulding young writers. With hindsight the contract may seem a little harsh."

Exploitative is a better word, thought Aggie. And a knack for spotting desperation. Her first novel had been rejected by countless publishers before it came to land on Edith's desk.

"Just remember all that she's given you. You signed up for fame, not fortune. One more novel and then you're free to go to any publishing house in the country. Don't tell me that they're not already queuing up?"

Aggie looked down guiltily. Of course they were. Editors and agents had been taking her to one side at literary events for "quiet little chats" ever since her first book hit the best seller lists. She'd watched as each subsequent novel rose through the numbered shelves in WH Smiths until it had become routine.

"My advice is: write that final novel and get out. But don't tell Edith I told you!" He winked as he let his hand fall lightly over hers across the hotel's tea room table.

God, they're all vultures! Aggie thought as she withdrew her hand as subtly as she could, feigning wiping her eyes with a heavily-starched napkin. Tears, he liked good old-fashioned tears. Delicate, ladylike tears to be dabbed away by cotton, lace-edged handkerchiefs. Not the red-faced tears of rage she had cried, alone in her flat, when she'd found out about Edith's sole claim to any production rights. It wasn't just the books that her dear editor owned, but any artistic interpretation of the work: radio, TV, theatre, graphic novels, tote bags, mugs, T-shirts, you name it. The small print had crept off the end of the contract like so many tiny ants.

The lawyer's response made Aggie regret wasting her time getting dressed up for the occasion. She usually lived in her pyjamas, tracksuits and hoodies; anything vaguely clean and comfortable that she could pull on without any fuss then sit down to her writing. She'd pop on trainers and a waterproof jacket for her twice-daily "brisk walks" and didn't really think of wearing anything else, except for when she had to be "A.M. West", successful crime writer in the classical style. So now she was freshly showered and sporting her trademark vintage look. She was wearing a tea dress, no less, with tan stockings and Mary Jane shoes. There was a string of pearls at her neck and a cashmere cardigan around her shoulders. Her hair was bobbed and straightened and her mouth painted blood red, as were her nails. She looked the picture of a lady taking afternoon tea in the 1930s, but she felt she might as well have turned up in her old jeans and hoodie, for all the good it was doing her!

The tea rooms at the Grand Hotel were exactly the kind of place Aggie had imagined Mr. Layfield-Brookes took Edith's distraught young female - or as he would say, "lady" - authors when they realised that they had been hoodwinked. The Grand served afternoon tea with all the essential accoutrements of the ritual: the tables were clothed in starched white tablecloths, the china was fine, the silver sparkling and it went without saying that there was a pianist playing light classical favourites. All was calm and civilised. Layfield-Brookes was also calm and civilised - as well as knowing, concerned and smug! Yes, under his old-world chivalry, the invitations to tea, the opening of doors, he was smug. He'd played his part in sequestering quite a clutch of naive young things in Edith's literary workhouse. She wondered how many had cried a little as he patted them on the hands, offered sympathy and the promise of help if they climbed the grand staircase to one of the hotel's sumptuous bedrooms for a more intimate tête-à-tête? Surely not! Not this skeleton in too-slack skin and a shabby suit! That had always been her problem: letting her imagination run away with her.

"But the television series!" she blurted out a little too loudly above the tinkling of the ivories, the clink of the china, and the hushed gossip.

"Let her have the rights to the series. You can insist on having the sole rights to your next one."

Aggie looked down again and signed, wishing he'd offer some form of help other than tea and sympathy. But following him up the stairs fortunately wasn't on the cards. She could use the idea for a novel about a literary agent who tricks a desperate young novelist into signing an exploitative contract. He then blackmails her into an unwanted romantic liaison in return for her release. When he goes back on his word she stabs him in the back with an ice pick from the ice bucket of the champagne he orders every time they meet at the Grand Hotel. No, it was too obvious! She'd have to come up with something better than a crime of passion. Something more complex and intriguing; a properly planned murder that involved at least two or three bodies, just like the old crime novels she so admired. How did those authors do it? How did they conjure up plot after baffling plot, year after year? Her problem was she was running out of ideas. The greats had written dozens, if not hundreds, of stories. Yet she wondered if she had one more novel in her, let alone another series. She seriously doubted whether she could even start number thirteen and be released from this Hadean contract.

"I know it's hard, my dear, but you're almost there. Just one more to go."

The waiter had brought the bill. Aggie reached for it, thinking at least she'd make a show of paying her way.

"No, no. You must allow me."

"But I've taken your time and professional advice." Not that it was what she had wanted to hear, and she suspected it was biased in Edith's favour. She also knew by now that the talk of "other publishers" was just mentioned to create the impression that she was free to make a choice. She suspected that he had her next contract lined up and she would be persuaded that she really couldn't do without Edith's extensive experience as an agent and editor. But of course she was free to go to any publishing house in the country, to any television company on the face of the earth, if only she was willing to take that risk.

"No, really, I insist. I just hope a little tea and cake has cheered you up a bit. And perhaps given you fuel for number thirteen?"

Yes, you're Edith's flunky after all, she thought. It's all about getting the writers back to the grindstone.

They took their leave at Grand Hotel's suitably imposing stone balustrade, the lawyer gallantly offering to hail her a taxi and kissing her on both cheeks. What century was he from? She said she preferred to walk, that it was good for inspiration.

He nodded. "That's the spirit, my girl!"

1,2,3,4,5,6,7,8,9,10,11,12,13

But really she was avoiding going back to her flat, desk, blank notebooks and even blanker computer screen. She couldn't for the life
210

of her think of a new plot. She had a good mind to kill off the stupid, frumpy little detective with the antiquated modes of speech and genteel accent she had invented what seemed like a lifetime ago. But this meant that she'd have to think of motive, means and opportunity in order to do it, and she'd pretty much done them all. The motives were mostly money or love. There had been a couple of plots centreing on murder over inheritances and the changing of wills. Some of her murders had been acts of revenge or responses to blackmail. People did still have a strong sense of shame, at least that wasn't anachronistic; there had been one or two snooty reviews over the years pulling her up for being "out of touch with the times". Critics had been pretty scathing about novel number seven where the murderer had been denied a divorce by her horror of a husband who was stopping her from running away with her younger lover. She had to admit that this one had been a bit unbelievable in these days where divorce and lovers were no longer taboo, but her readers had lapped it up.

The means had been amply covered: bludgeoning, stabbing, shooting, drowning, and poisoning – yes, there had been quite a bit of poisoning. Poisoning was fine in the Golden Age of crime fiction, when poisons had been readily available and difficult to trace in autopsies but now you couldn't exactly go into Boots and ask for some arsenic. But then again, her readers didn't seem to mind, and her faithful little detective always came through. She was guaranteed to see through the usual red herrings which covered up opportunity: the watch broken at the supposed time of the murder, guaranteeing an alibi; the spotting of a suspect in a nearby town or of a tramp wandering the grounds of the country manor (disguises); overheard snatches of conversation (recordings) by the housekeeper (now the hourly-paid Eastern European contract cleaner), which meant that a suspect couldn't possibly have been at the scene of the crime. And so the clues or non-clues went on, spotted by her heroine's unassuming yet eagle eyes: the traces of glue on a suspect's chin (for the fake beard, of course); the overplayed accents (Romanian cleaning ladies don't really sound like Dracula, now do they, dear reader?); the fragments of a document found in the ashes of a wood-burning stove (it would usually have been in a fire, but she did do some nods to middle-class modernity); footprints in the flowerbeds or snow. Footprints in the snow were central to her special Christmas short story, written out of contract. Edith had somehow persuaded her to write it: "Think of the honour, and the publicity, to be published in The Times Christmas Supplement!" Aggie would have preferred The Guardian, but she knew her material wasn't left-field enough.

She had run through the tried and tested tropes of: the least likely suspect being the murderer; the seemingly impossible "locked room mystery"; the "closed circle of suspects" scenario (country houses, trains and cruise ships); and the case solved by the armchair detective (her little lady had been laid low with the flu). She had the usual identity and name changes, even though with Facebook and Instagram it was now very difficult to disappear for years and then appear as someone else. She'd hoped, however, that the he-to-she change in novel five had given it a contemporary feel.

And so she had carved out her niche in this, her chosen and time-honoured genre. Perhaps she wasn't quite the new "Queen of Crime", but she was fêted as "breathing new life into a classic craft" and praised for regaling her fans with "good old-fashioned crime for today's readers". Her plots were faster-paced, characters less cardboard and settings more atmospheric than those of the canon. Modern readers weren't given to having to do a lot of work to fill out characters or to figure out who done it. "A modern twist on classic crime" was her strapline.

She had gone by the book up until now but as the proverb went (and she had used quite a few of those in her novels, as well as nursery rhymes, to classically chilling effect): "it is the last straw that breaks the camel's back." That was what the TV deal was. It was Edith's casual mention of it, almost in passing, that hurt the most. "Oh and the Beeb has been in touch about adapting our novels." That, and the "our". Aggie knew she would have no part in the deal, no influence in the adaptation or dramatization. There would be no reviewing scripts or hanging out on set with famous actors. Edith would claim that "the author didn't want to influence a distinct art form", or that she had a migraine or whatever. And of course, there would be no money.

She should just follow Layfield-Brookes' advice, write the final novel in her contract, and then negotiate her own deal with publishers and broadcasters for the next series. She imagined delicious scraps between the BBC and the other channels, while her cut would be rising. But she had a sinking feeling that, without Edith to poke and prod her, she would never even get novel number thirteen started. She knew that she wouldn't be able to produce another series, not without Edith there to edit her "incoherent ramblings". Edith's description had been hurtful, but after so long working together, Aggie believed her. Without the hope of another series, she'd be left with very little to show for over a decade of living in the same damp flat, dedicating her every waking hour to detective fiction. This was the final straw, the nail in the coffin. The straw that broke the camel's back.

She was back in her flat in no time, her anger must have made her power-walk. She had no memory of the route back from the Grand, through the increasingly grimy streets to her upper flat in a crumbling Victorian terrace. Almost thirteen bestsellers and she was still living in this dump! She had rented the flat when she was a penniless writer, surviving on a part time job in a coffee shop, before that fateful day when she met Edith Mulgrave. She was still living there, she didn't have the money or energy to move. Edith's writing schedule was all-consuming. She longed for the days when she would scribble in her notebook whenever inspiration took her, or type up her notes in her favourite coffee shop. She would inevitably spend more time chatting to fellow writers in that bohemian niche which served coffee far superior and more ethically-produced than the generic stuff served at the high street chain where she worked. But she put all the hours she spent "hanging out" down to being an essential part of the artistic process.

1,2,3,4,5,6,7,8,9,10,11,12,13

Since meeting Edith, she had become a machine: her plots were meticulously mapped out before writing, characters sketched and significant names dreamt up, locations described in detail, each chapter's hook to the next clearly indicated. Her days had taken on aspects of a military regime. She was at her desk at seven am, revising the writing from the day before. There would be a coffee and croissant break at nine and then she'd continue writing new material until midday, when she'd have a quick sandwich and a walk to clear her exhausted head. She might squeeze another hour or two out of her tired brain and fingers if the fresh air had given her some inspiration. The rest of the afternoon was spent interacting with her fans. Edith insisted that maintaining a web presence was just as important as producing the "goods", as she called them. She had a website and Facebook and Twitter accounts, and these all needed to be attended to. Her fans were really devoted and she had to be equally dedicated to them. She'd heard from other writers she'd met at literary festivals that their agents arranged for "communication officers" to manage this side of their careers, but Edith would have none of it:

"Your fans want you, my dear. Always remember that they put you where you are now! If they're willing to waste their time reading your rubbish, then the least you can do is to spend a little time on theirs!"

Aggie left feeling guilty but deep down knew it was all about saving money. From then on, Edith always watched her like a hawk at literary events, steering her away from other authors.

Then there were all the festivals, readings, signings and book launches to attend. She'd thought it would be glamorous, sitting in her writers' café before she was famous, but it was work, so much work. Before, her dreams of becoming a famous writer had involved living in a big Georgian house in the nice part of town, her study filled with wall-to-ceiling bookshelves. And of course she'd have a flat in London for all those visits to her editors and catching those flights to exotic locations for research. When Aggie had suggested setting a novel abroad, hoping for a research trip, Edith insisted that "home territory" was what the fans liked and Wikipedia was good enough for research. But now, most of all she dreamt of writing for herself in her old coffee shop. But she couldn't go back in there. Whenever she'd tried to reconnect with her old writer friends over the over-priced cappuccinos, there would always be someone who recognised her and asked for her autograph, or asked what the plot for the next novel would be, or that they disagreed with her on the solution in novel number six.

And then there was always the pedantic fan who just didn't get artistic licence. They would point out that vials of morphine were registered with the NHS and if you bought them on the street for £25 a shot (yes, they agreed that this was the going price) they could still be traced back to the issuing hospital. They would calmly inform her that simply swapping morphine for insulin didn't really wash because the police would ask where the morphine had come from. They would be able to trace the morphine back to the hospital, to the homeless person who needed it for his cancer, then onwards to the guy who stole it from him, and then to the nice middle-class lady who fitted the description of Aunt Dolly who stood to gain half a million once she had knocked her diabetic husband off, even though her own life seemed to be in danger. Aggie hardly had the energy to point out that the labels on the vials of morphine had been exchanged for those of insulin and that she had checked, the bottles would have looked exactly the same. Anyway, only her little detective could spot a clue like that and trace the chain back, through her chance conversation with Tony, a homeless friend of hers for whom she bought cups of tea and the occasional doughnut. He had mentioned he had had his medication stolen and that was the beginning of the detective's dénouement. Her readers surely knew by now that the police wouldn't be able to come up with all that! Fortunately, Edith was a supreme pedant and had taught her well, insisting that she check every little detail. This mostly did the trick of pre-empting her more ardent, detail-obsessed fans.

"Always remember that they're cleverer than you are, my dear. They see from the outside in, whereas you see from the inside out."

Aggie had to admit, painfully, that she was, as always, right.

1,2,3,4,5,6,7,8,9,10,11,12,13

She remembered the fateful day clearly when she met Edith Mulgrave for the first time. It had marked a turning point in her life. She'd read somewhere that people recall seminal moments in their lives in great and unnecessary detail: the warm breeze on their skin just before the explosion, the clanging of a tinny tune on a teenager's headphones before the train crash, the buzzing of a bluebottle in the doctor's surgery before the breaking of bad news. For Aggie, it was the cold damp of the corridor as she shut the door on the blustery autumn afternoon outside, the further drop in temperature as she entered the high-ceilinged, musty room at 37A Nicolson Street. She'd seen an advert in the café, a small plastic pocket filled with unassuming business cards, pinned to the noticeboard which was overpopulated with flyers for yoga classes, acoustic open mic nights and language exchanges. She took one and the little, cream-coloured card spoke to her instantly:

"Aspiring writers wanted! Tired of rejection letters? Or of no response at all?

Send your manuscripts to:

Miss Edith Mulgrave, editor, agent and publisher at:

Morning Star Publishers

37A Nicolson Street,

Newfort,

NE1 6FZ.

Only printed, posted manuscripts accepted*.

216

Please include your postal address for replies.

You are only a postage stamp away from becoming a publishing sensation!

Double line spaced, wide margins and printed on one side only, please."

Aggie had thought it odd at the time, that there was no email address, website or phone number. And the thing about including a postal address. Who did that these days? It all seemed so old-fashioned. But, then again, perhaps that was the appeal. You couldn't just ignore a four hundred page manuscript when it came through your letterbox. Or rather, when the postman knocked at your door because it wouldn't fit through the letterbox. You couldn't just press Delete, could you? But then again, who was she trying to fool? A printed manuscript would be just as easy to leave on a desk, unread, or to be dumped in the waste paper basket. And she'd have to pay for the printing and postage. She'd need more than one stamp to send in her poor, much-rejected novel. But somehow it seemed more possible. That little business card gave her hope. She carried it around with her for a couple of weeks while she debated what to do.

1,2,3,4,5,6,7,8,9,10,11,12,13

Looking back, spying that business card came at just the right time. The coffee shop had offered her more hours and sitting sipping hand-crafted cappuccinos and writing had its price. Just as she was about to take on more barista work, work that could easily have become full-time, for the rest of her life, taking her away from her true calling, an envelope landed in the entranceway of her shared building. It was from another time: the paper was heavy, deeply-textured and watermarked, the same ivory colour as the business card. Her address was etched into its deep unctuous pile with the rapid, uneven stabs of a typewriter. Aggie was intrigued as she weighed the envelope in her hands while she climbed the stairs to her upper flat. She felt that it needed to be opened with a proper letter opener, or at least a knife, not ripped messily apart with her fingers. She sensed that this would be important. Once in her flat she dug out a butter knife, carefully opened the envelope and took the letter out. It was set out in the old-fashioned style that she had learned at school: her address, the date, Dear Miss Agatha Miller. And then the main body, the letters cut deep into the paper's tissue, but cutting deeper into Aggie's heart:

"Having read the manuscript you so kindly sent, we feel your writing shows real promise. As an independent publishing house dedicated to discovering and nurturing new talent, we would welcome the opportunity of meeting to discuss future possibilities for collaboration. We would be delighted if you would be so kind as to present yourself at our offices on Monday, 30th of October at 4 pm.

Yours sincerely,

Miss Edith Mulgrave,

Editor, Agent and Publisher,

Morning Star Publishers,

37A Nicolson Street,

Newfort,

NE1 6FZ."

It was already getting dark as she stood outside the blackened Georgian row on the derelict square. Damp leaves dogged her best shoes, which were not really practical for a night like this. She pulled the old-fashioned doorbell and heard it clang around what seemed like an empty building. She waited. No one answered. She wondered if she'd got the wrong address. She fished around in her coat pockets for the business card. She peered at it in the gloom, then up at the plaque of the street name, lit by a miserable street lamp, and the number of the building, half-hidden in the fading light. This was the place, alright. She tried the bell again, listened intently as it clanged around the cavernous interior. Listened for the footsteps which didn't come. What about the date? The time? Had she got these wrong? She rummaged in her bag for the letter. The damned thing wouldn't open! And now it was starting to rain. Ugh! Finally, she got it out. No. It was there clearly enough: "Monday, 30th of October at 4 pm." It was definitely the 30th, her writer friends were having a ghost story event at the café tomorrow evening. She checked her watch. It had just turned four. She had arrived early for once. She decided to try the bell one more time and then go home. Perhaps it had all been some kind of a joke. One of the disgruntled writers at the café having a laugh. Then, just as she was about to turn away, the door opened a crack. She pushed at it tentatively. There was no one there.

It was colder and damper inside the dark hallway than on the doorstep. She wondered if anyone was in the building at all. The office workers must have left early, to get home before the weather turned really bad. There was a storm brewing. She saw a line of light from under a doorway, and spied out a brass plate, glowing in the gloom: Morning Star Publishers. She knocked tentatively, and was greeted with a booming

"Entrez!"

As she pushed open the heavy, creaking door, she felt a gust of wind sucking her inward, which she would later recall as feeling like her soul was being sucked out of her. It was in fact a vacuum caused by the window being open, even on a night like this. It transpired that Edith was a smoker, constantly surrounded by the fug of her cheroots, and always had the window open, whatever the weather. It was her imagination getting the better of her, as always. She made out a small spidery figure hunched behind a large mahogany desk, piled high with papers and manuscripts. The spider's hair was greying and artistically wild. A paisley pashmina was flung around her shoulders. She looked at Aggie over her half-moon spectacles and indicated the chair in front of her with a majestic sweep of her hand. Her wizened fingers were stained with nicotine and encrusted with burnished gold rings, her nails pointed talons painted blood red. She had a glass of red wine in one hand and a cigarette in the other.

"Do sit down. Will you?" Edith offered her a glass of wine.

Aggie politely refused.

"Don't drink?"

"Not really."

"Good, good. I've had enough of writers with drink problems. It's good to keep a clear head. Now, down to business. This manuscript of yours."

Aggie looked down at her hands red from making coffee and fingernails bitten from nervously pondering plots.

"It's very much the stuff of fanzine, now isn't it?"

Aggie's heart dropped. It sounded very much like the one piece of feedback she'd had from an editor; that her novel was "derivative". Most hadn't bothered with feedback at all.

"I can see that you're an admirer of the classic detective novel."

"Well, yes, yes, I'm a big fan of the Golden Age," Aggie stammered.

"I can see that."

Aggie didn't know if this was good or bad.

"But I'm pleased to say that I think that this novel has potential."

Aggie's heart fluttered, like a butterfly about to be trapped in the paws of a particularly sadistic cat. Looking back, that's what this, and subsequent interviews had been like, a cat playing with a butterfly, letting her soar, only to knock her down.

"Yes, you're a writer, alright. You definitely have the gift."

Aggie's heart missed a beat. She was soaring.

"Now, what if I were to suggest that you set this piece of fan mail in the twenty-first century? Give it a more contemporary feel? I mean detective novels set in the thirties have been done to death. Forgive the pun."

Bang! The paw slammed down.

"I..."

"Now, I've taken the liberty of making some notes for changes I feel will make this novel publishable."

Edith handed Aggie her manuscript. It was completely covered in spidery scribblings; in between the lines, in the margins, and right over onto the reverse side of the pages. It wasn't for nothing that she'd asked for it to be double line spaced and with wide margins, and printed on one side only!

"Well, not only published, but a success - a bestseller!"

Aggie was dumbfounded. It was as though her precious novel was covered in battle scars! But the thought of being published, of seeing her words in a printed book, of being read, after so many rejections, had her heart singing.

"Now, you run along and make the changes, send me the revised draft in, say, a month's time, and then we'll talk about further editing and a contract."

"I..."

Aggie felt like saying that she didn't feel like making any changes, that this was her novel and -

221

"Oh yes, of course, how silly of me. You'll be wanting an advance. I wouldn't want a talent like yours wasted serving those nasty little high-street chain cappuccinos. No, of course not! That just wouldn't do!"

Later, Aggie wondered how she knew about the coffee shop. But then again, a lot of writers worked in cafés, didn't they?

"Here, now you take this."

Edith reached into one of her deep drawers and extracted a cheque book - I mean, who has those these days? - and wrote a cheque for £1000.

"But, don't you want some sort of guarantee? I mean ..."

"You mean you could just run off with the money?"

"Yes."

"I trust you."

Edith's eyes glinted red. It was almost a threat.

1,2,3,4,5,6,7,8,9,10,11,12,13

Aggie's days were filled with editing. She became obsessed with tracing the spider's web of notes as though they were threads of a mystery. She called in sick at work. After all, she had that cheque. She hardly left her flat, imagining herself to be a proper writer now, spending hours a day at her computer screen, living with her characters, working through the rewriting. It was a substantial task. It was not so much the plot that needed work, but the updating of the settings, the characters and their motivations. She was beginning to realise that society had changed since the 1930s, as had social interactions and indicators of class. Well, the hierarchies still existed, it was just that they were dressed up differently. Edith had perceptively noted in a margin that it would be good to keep in these references to class as readers, especially American readers, loved the British class system. At a later interview Edith had confidently claimed:

"We're going for the American market, my dear. So much bigger than a strictly UK audience. And you don't have to pay translators. Just get good old Robert in our New York office to check it all through, change a few words and spellings, and Bob's your uncle. Forgive the pun!"

It was touches like this that made Aggie trust Edith. She had faith in her experience, in her knowledge of the market and of what readers wanted. In the midst of her frantic rewriting, she ventured out to her coffee shop, excited to share her news with her writer friends. She realised immediately it was a mistake. There were remarks about "commercialisation" and "selling out" from one particularly bohemian "friend" (though everyone knew she herself was living off a trust fund). Others made concerned comments about her lack of a contract, insisting that she made sure she got a lawyer when one did appear. They seemed to be clipping her wings and she left the café thinking that they were just jealous: she was well on her way to getting a writing contract, to being published, to being read by thousands if not millions of readers! And they were just sitting around sipping over-priced organic cappuccinos and reading the book reviews in The Guardian (though not of their own books!). She vowed never to go in there again. At least not until she was famous and could rub their jealous little noses in it!

1,2,3,4,5,6,7,8,9,10,11,12,13

By the time all the editing and re-editing was done (Edith had insisted on several rewrites), Aggie wondered how much of her original novel was left. She had been living off Edith's monthly advances and was still waiting to discuss her contract when her first novel was published, and to much acclaim: it leaped into the Richard and Judy Book Club, and her heart missed a beat or two as she saw copies of it piled high in WH Smiths. There were book signings, readings, and a whole whirlwind of social events. Aggie felt giddy with fame. She would have signed a contract in blood if she had to. But she knew Edith had made that book what it was, that she needed her.

The trap had been sprung, the cat's paw went down.

Bang!

The contract arrived in the post, in one of Edith's classic, creamy envelopes. It was heavy, full of small print and language Aggie didn't understand. But she knew that if she wanted this to continue, to be more than fifteen minutes of fame, she would have to sign. And sign she did. It would mean that she'd get her fair share of royalties, wouldn't it?

Then the letter arrived, her address etched deeply into the thick, watermarked parchment. It seemed overly formal, with the "Miss" and the royal "we", coming from someone with whom she had worked so closely. But then, that was the point, part of the cat-and-butterfly game that only later did she realise they were playing.

"Dear Miss Agatha Miller,

We would like to take this opportunity to congratulate you in writing on the successful reception of our first novel. We think you will agree that its success is due to our fruitful collaboration.

We must also comment on your wise decision to sign the contract we so generously offered you, which we are at pains to remind you included our first novel. Trademarking our pen-name "A.M. West" was also a good decision. All smart moves which will guarantee you fame, if not fortune, in the world of crime publishing.

However, we must not rest on our laurels. The first draft of our next novel is due in three months' time. We are placing you under a strict schedule in order that you comply with the terms of our contract, of producing a novel a year for the next twelve years."

Aggie gasped. She had thought that she'd have a year to write a novel, but no - Edith's next line seemed to have read her mind.

"By this of course we mean that we will publish, rather than write, a novel a year. You will send me the manuscript in three months' time and we will write in due course to set the time and date of our next interview.

Please find enclosed a cheque for £3000, your advance on the manuscript.

Looking forward to reading your sequel.*

Yours sincerely,

Miss Edith Mulgrave.

*It needs to be a sequel with that little lady detective character of yours centre stage. Readers will be wanting more of the same. We don't want any nasty surprises, now do we? It's all in your contract, if you would care to read it."

A sick feeling came over her, from the pit of her stomach. She had to write another novel from scratch in three months? That first novel had been years in the making, years of dreaming and stopping and starting, of being distracted by short story and poetry competitions, of attending reading events which had all been so much part of the artistic process. And now Edith wanted another one in three months! The contract had said a novel a year, not in three months, surely? She rummaged in her desk drawers for the damned thing! And there it was, in black and white, with her signature on the bottom, in fancy fountain pen, which could have just as easily been blood. She could see its rusty brown hue, smell its metallic odour.

"I, the undersigned, promise to publish a novel a year for the next twelve years solely with Morning Star Publishing House, Ltd. I agree to be paid by monthly advance for my services to the above stated company. All rights and royalties are to remain with the company."

1,2,3,4,5,6,7,8,9,10,11,12,13

So Aggie had sat down to write. She had written and published a novel a year for the last twelve years. She had left on the shelf her dreams of her great novel, the one that would be reviewed by the Guardian, be shortlisted for the Mann Booker and be included on university syllabuses. It was true that Edith had sucked the fortune out of her writing, but in one more novel's time, she would be free. Free to go to any publishing house in the country and ask for a substantial advance on this great novel of hers! But equally well did she know that it was Edith that had made the novels into the success that they were. Edith knew what their readers wanted. Time and again, Aggie had opened her Twitter feed to see a rapturous comment about some touch or twist that Edith had suggested in her spidery notes. She knew that she couldn't do it on her own, that other publishing houses wouldn't be interested in a novel by Aggie Miller. They only wanted A.M. West. Edith had even invented her pen-name for her. She had insisted on something that could be either masculine or feminine. She was of the opinion that more old-fashioned readers might have more respect for male writers, despite there being a long line of "Queens of Crime".

"No, no, no my dear! Aggie Miller just won't do! People might think it's a romantic novel. No, we want something that denotes crime, and nothing but crime. And something that appeals to both male and female readers. We're going for sales here. The customer is always right, remember."

Aggie hadn't been in a position to disagree. She had never disagreed.

1,2,3,4,5,6,7,8,9,10,11,12,13

In the early years, Aggie had somehow found the time to work on her "own stuff". She would scribble away in stolen moments and type up the results until late at night. "After her working hours" was how she justified this shirking of responsibilities to herself. Then, after much tortured deliberation, she dared to present the manuscript that she hoped would become "her great novel" to Edith, with a casual

"Perhaps you could take a look at this, it's not my usual thing, but…"

Edith stared stonily at her from above her half-moon specs.

"We have a contract. You promised to complete thirteen crime novels with a certain female detective as the star. I do hope you haven't been getting distracted, my dear. I was wondering about book four, it did seem a little light to me. And now I can see why. Good books require discipline. Word after word, sentence after sentence, page after page, chapter after chapter."

"I know, but it *is* a novel and I wrote it in my spare time, it's _"

Aggie was cut off with a raised hand, indicating "Enough" without Edith having to say a word.

"I don't think I need to tell you that you shouldn't have any "spare time". I'm not against the taking of brisk walks to gain inspiration or to work on particularly knotty bits of plot. No, they're all part of the process. But to work on other writing, well, that's just a distraction. We have a tight schedule, writing in the morning and early afternoon, social media and keeping the fans happy in the afternoon. A couple of brisk walks in between and early to bed with a cup of coco. No excuses! I had one young writer who tried to claim that going out to the pub was "research". It didn't end well for him, I can tell you!"

Edith left that thought hanging in the air as her eyes flared red. Aggie wondered what dreadful thing had befallen the young writer. What could be so bad? Not to get published? Not to have to sit at the computer screen day after day squeezing your brain in and out of tortuous plots? Of trying to find practical solutions to technical problems; perhaps a change of tense would do the trick, or a different adverb? Of living out your characters' pain and demons? Of suffering Edith's spidery comments? Rewriting. It was the rewriting that was the killer. But for some reason she imagined the young man slumped over his laptop, a knife in his back, or lying stone cold on the floor of his damp little bedsit, his body and handsome young face cast in agony, a tumbler of whiskey clenched in his contorted fist.

Edith glanced at the manuscript derisively.

"A romantic novel, by the looks of things. For goodness sake, Agatha! A.M. West does not write romantic novels. She writes crime. Her readers expect crime, not romantic fluff!"

Aggie stammered:

"But it's not a romantic novel per se… Well, it does flirt with the genre, or rather subverts it. It's really my testament to the state of post-modern womanhood in the tradition of Jane Aus-"

A wizened hand went up again.

"It looks as though you have The Guardian review written already."

The sarcasm cut through Aggie like one of the incredibly sharp kitchen knives her characters employed in their cold-hearted murder.

Edith sighed. Rather theatrically, Aggie thought.

"It's just not what readers expect from A. M. West, now is it?"

Aggie made one last-ditch attempt at protest, one that she would never repeat:

"But what about Aggie Miller?"

Edith paused for dramatic effect and stared at Aggie blankly.

"Who's she?"

1,2,3,4,5,6,7,8,9,10,11,12,13

Before Edith, when Aggie hung out with the artistic crowd at her coffee shop, she had tried hard to emulate their mismatched chic. She dressed in her charity shop "finds", which she liked to think had a "vintage twist". But she knew that she never quite pulled it off, she was never quite in with the hipster crowd. She was always on the fringes, the shy girl looking in from the outside, observing. It was Edith who had developed her look as "A.M. West"; her trademark tweeds which were a nod to another era. She'd bought Aggie an expensive wardrobe of dogtooth-patterned skirts, tailored jackets, cashmere twin sets, Mary Jane shoes and thick leather brogues. She'd had Aggie have her long hair cut into a smooth bob. She insisted that she wear blood red lipstick, like a slash across her face, and paint her nails a matching shade for all her public events. The pearls had been a gift for the phenomenal success of novel number three. Edith had invited Layfield-Brookes and Aggie for a champagne supper at the Dorchester after the London book launch. She passed the vintage jewellery case across the table with: "To complete your transformation, Miss A.M. West. They were my mother's." Aggie was surprised to hear that Edith had a mother! Her trademark diamond-encrusted spider brooch had been a gift for novel number five. Aggie watched as sales for copies of the piece of jewellery had soared. Edith knew her marketing, alright. As Aggie left the unfortunate interview about her own beloved "stuff", she caught her reflection in the hallway mirror and realised that her transformation from Aggie Miller, the shy and sensitive coffee shop writer, to the confident and mysterious crime novelist, A.M. West, was complete.

1,2,3,4,5,6,7,8,9,10,11,12,13

After that painful episode, Aggie swore never to cross Edith again, and they fell back into their rhythm of draft and redraft, book launches and festivals. They were like a well-oiled machine. However, as Aggie was about to start the final novel under her contract, she found that Edith was getting a little jumpy, and their interviews more tense.

"You won't do anything silly, now. Will you, my dear?"

Aggie looked down at her hands, contemplating either suicide or murder.

"What on earth do you mean, Edith?"

(They were now on first name terms. It had taken a few years and had been instigated by Edith: "But come now, after all these years, you can surely call me Edith!")

"You know exactly what I mean. Writers tend to become reckless when they're running out of ideas."

Aggie looked down at her hands again, and bit her tongue.

"I mean, your detective, so beloved by your readers, has been developing heart problems due to consuming too many chocolate eclairs. All well and good, it creates a sense of suspense. And of course we've been encouraging the rumour that this might just be our last novel. Sales are set to soar. Readers are already desperate to know whether or not you're going to kill her off. But you're not going to. Do you hear me?"

Aggie nodded.

"Now, you run along and get to work. The Beeb has been in touch about adapting our novels. They'll be wanting to know that the final one is in hand. And that will be season one. We'll have to start thinking about another thirteen novels for season two, and that will mean an even quicker turnaround. None of the luxury of a novel a year. No, we'll really have to get a move on. Oh, and of course we'll have to discuss your next contract."

Aggie left the interview stunned. The BBC? A television series? Another thirteen books? Another contract? When she got home she riffled through her papers for her contract and called Layfield-Brookes. He had then invited her to their disappointing rendezvous at the Grand.

Their interview over afternoon tea hadn't been helpful.

Or had it?

"The straw that broke the camel's back".

Capitalise it and it became the title of a novel.

Her last novel with Edith.

Their final novel.

She opened her notebook, and began to write as though her life depended on it.

1,2,3,4,5,6,7,8,9,10,11,12,13

They met three months later, on a stormy autumn evening not dissimilar to the one when they'd first met, nearly thirteen years ago. The office was dark, save for the table lamp, and a freezing breeze swept into the room from behind the heavy velvet curtains. Aggie had brought a bottle of red wine - not merely a gift for Edith; Aggie had started to drink herself. It was the only way she could get to sleep after all the coffee and staring at the screen - and this she served with her back turned to her editor at a side table by the empty fireplace. She placed Edith's glass by her elbow, while she kept her own in her hand. She kept quiet, refrained from making a toast, and waited for Edith to speak. Edith always spoke first, and on this occasion, Aggie hoped to build some suspense by staring pointedly at Edith's glass of Merlot.

"I must say I'm glad you've got over your writer's block and your silly little quibbles over our contract."

Layfield-Brookes had obviously told her about their afternoon tea appointment. Aggie reverted to examining her nails and biting her tongue.

"The first scene is arresting, as always. The literary agent-cum-editor found slumped over her desk, a glass of red wine spilt all over her papers, is well-drawn. All in all it's nicely paced. If I've taught you one thing over the years I'd like to think it's how to soldier your uncontrolled ramblings into a finely-tuned structure. The motive, means and opportunity are all played through well, with plenty of misleading lines of enquiry, as is the wont of classic crime fiction. You have a solid line-up of the usual suspects: the young novelist who feels hard-done by an exploitative contract (she has an alibi, she was at a book signing attended by at least two hundred fans at a Waterstones in a town at least an hour away by train); the long-lost son who comes back to claim his inheritance (again, he has an alibi, he didn't come back into the country until a week after the murder and he has his flight tickets to prove it); the neurotic young author who has had one too many rejection letters and who has no alibi for the night in question. Then you have your red and not-so-red herrings: there is the tramp seen lurking around the square near the editor's office (could that be the son in disguise?); the raised voices heard by the upstairs office staff a couple of days before the editor's body is found, and a young woman who is seen running down the steps, face turned downwards, possibly in tears - it is raining and the woman is shielded by an umbrella - could it have been the established writer or the new recruit?.

Well, motive and means are solid, and as for opportunity, you know the rest, my dear."

At this point, Edith looked intently at her wine glass, but didn't raise it to her lips.

"I must say, however, on a personal note, that I think you're rather harsh in your depiction of the editor. The description of her as some kind of wizened old crone is rather cliché. I thought you could have been more original in your depiction of evil old ladies. And it's really not very realistic to represent the contract in any way as "exploitative". It's quite usual for publishers to retain quite a high percentage of the profits of book sales, given all the work we do. And in this case I do think the agent is very generous in her terms and conditions. After all, paying out advances to unknown authors is quite a risk. And to commit to a relationship of thirteen books? Unheard of!"

Aggie could take no more, the straw had broken the camel's back.

"But the TV rights! Edith, really, I'm only asking you to be reasonable!"

She immediately regretted losing her temper. She had imagined creating an atmosphere of fear through controlled silence. Just like her villains, she thought she would have been cool, suave and pathologically unemotional. She fell silent and stared at Edith's still-untouched glass of red wine. She passed over the papers in which she set out an amendment to her existing contract, to allow her fifty percent of the broadcasting rights. She thought that fair enough.

"I suggest you sign," she said as coolly as she could, staring meaningfully at the wine.

There was no reaction. Just an awkward silence. Edith didn't even glance at the papers.

"You know how the story ends," Aggie added with as much menace as she could muster.

"Or, rather, begins, my dear." Edith began to laugh.

"What's so funny?"

"You've always done everything by the book!"

Aggie sat, deflated and embarrassed. This wasn't how she'd imagined her final showdown with her long-time nemesis.

Edith rummaged in her deep drawer, and produced her own document, entitled "The Last Will and Testament of Miss Edith Mulgrave." She tossed the manila folder over to Aggie and raised her glass with a "Cheers" and a wink. She took a sip.

"Mmm, nice Merlot. Not your usual plonk."

Aggie looked on in disbelief. Edith tossed her head back and laughed a half-hysterical cackle.

"I don't care if it does kill me, although I doubt that it will. We both know that you can't get arsenic over the counter these days, and they don't put it in rat poison anymore. Facts that our dear readers seem happy to ignore out of - who coined it? Coleridge? - willing suspension of disbelief. Or just plain stupidity."

Aggie nodded. Of course she hadn't poisoned the wine. It was all done for dramatic effect. Thirteen years of writing detective novels in the old-school style had taken their toll. She looked down at the will.

"I, the undersigned, leave all my worldly goods (my office, literary agency, house out in the leafy suburbs, flat in London) and intellectual property (the rights to the agency's novels and any subsequent adaptations) to Miss Agatha Miller…"

"But why?"

"I'm not long for this world, you see. Not arsenic but nicotine. Prospero is breaking her rod, my dear."

Aggie sat stunned. She was Ariel soaring, free as a butterfly on a warm summer's day. She imagined unearthing her great novel, getting back to work on it at her old coffee shop and publishing it under her own name to much critical acclaim.

And then Edith called her back to earth: Bang!

"Of course you can recruit some "ghost writers", although I prefer to call them "apprentices", to work on your next series. I suggest you place adverts in coffee shops, that worked a treat for me. Layfield-Brookes can help you with the contracts. You'll need to consider confidentiality clauses. But you can discuss all that over afternoon tea at the Grand."

Edith's eyes flashed red. Aggie realised that she would never write anything ever again but spidery notes in the margins of other writers' manuscripts. With a dreadful sense of her fate, Aggie blurted:

"But why? Why me?"

"Because I too do everything by the book. Now, drink up, my dear."

The lawyer Layfield-Brookes and literary agent, publisher and editor extraordinaire Miss Agatha Miller met at the Grand to celebrate the success of series three. Aggie no longer sported the sleek retro look of A.M. West. She was now a banshee-cum-gypsy lady, her greying hair wiry and wild, burnished gold rings on her wizening, nicotine-stained fingers and a faded paisley pashmina around her hunching shoulders. Layfield-Brookes was even more of a skeleton in an even slacker suit. Bound to a wheelchair after a series of strokes, there would be no ascending the grand staircase to the sumptuous suites above the tearooms for him. Aggie had to admit that he had drawn up some hard-nosed contracts over the years, but they had always been in Morning Star Publishing's favour, and they had reaped the rewards. Their little lady detective still had a penchant for chocolate eclairs, still had that heart problem that kept her fans fretting over her imminent demise, but she still sleuthed on. Indeed, they all of them soldiered on, feeding the machine that had made them millionaires.

They ordered the champagne tea for two. There was much to celebrate, despite their increasing age and declining health. A.M. West had mysteriously disappeared from the literary circuit, to rumours and scandals that kept the myth alive, but sullied the novels' reputation. There had been much talk of "churning them out" and "ghost writers". But sales were still as strong as ever. So what did the critics know? The fans were loyal as ever. Setting one of the novels in an abandoned castle on the way to Oban had sparked rumours that their beloved author was living on the west coast of Scotland. Sightings had been made at the port which had boosted the town's tourist trade. Aggie toyed with the idea of making deals with unloved towns' Tourist Boards. Layfield-Brookes had even suggested the idea of creating an 'A.M West Trail', but they had been too busy overseeing the production of the novels, pursuing non-trademarked merchandise in the courts and managing the media to pursue such projects. The company wouldn't have really benefited anyway. And it was always about the company.

And then of course there were the TV series. Novel thirteen of series two had been completed nearly seven years ago. The BBC had almost banged down their door for the TV rights. There had been quite a battle going on between the standard channels. Series three had just been produced by Netflix. And now there was talk of a film, or indeed films. Aggie thought that perhaps Hollywood was calling a little late in the game, but still, those trips out to L.A. were always fun. She revelled in the stretched limos the size of that damp little flat where she'd written her first series, the cocktail parties by ornamental swimming pools, under skies so big and blue they made her dizzy, and the discussions in icy air-conditioned board rooms in chrome and glass buildings of which A-lister would play the leading lady. Aggie would never forget the day when Angelina Jolie walked into a meeting, all slender arms and legs and a smile that you needed sunglasses to look at. She would save that story for her memoir. But these Hollywood stars were all too unbelievably young and glamorous to play her frumpy little lady detective. She was still holding out for Judi Dench.

As they clinked their sparking Edinburgh crystal champagne flutes, they made their usual darkly witty references to cyanide. But who would benefit if one bumped the other off? They were locked together in an eternal dance of death of their souls. Aggie imagined two skeletons clinking their bones together in a macabre jive on the tearoom's dance floor. She still had it, that imagination. They nibbled at the delicate triangles of bread, butter and cucumber that symbolised sandwiches, chomped through the freshest of scones, Cornish clotted cream and homemade strawberry jam and leisurely worked their way up to the French dainties at the top of the cake stand. It was comforting to know that the Grand still served afternoon tea the way it should be - the pianist playfully tapping out light classics, the tablecloths starched stiff white, the china brittle as bones riddled with osteoporosis... Again Aggie's macabre imagination came out, she couldn't help it, the silverware a perfect mirror but...

But...

But the pianist occasionally dropped a note, or was ever-so-slightly out of key, striking a note of discord, of dread. The carpets under the tables were threadbare, scuffed by years of shunting chairs occupied by amble dowagers. The rococo plasterwork of the ceiling rose was covering a couple of well-turned-out old dears with a smattering of powder. Aggie wondered if they noticed the "icing sugar" covering their cakes, scones and sandwiches. The heavily florid wallpaper was peeling away in the alcoves, too heavy for the walls to bear. The waiters were slow, shuffling, stiffly polite, ready to pack up and retire to a reasonably priced nursing home by the sea, preferably somewhere on the south coast, where the Victorian terraces were whiter and the climate milder. But the seagulls would still scream out for scraps and shit on their cloth caps and overcoats. And the care workers would be surly and cold, only cosying up to the inhabitants if they thought they could get a look-in on an inheritance. No, these characters didn't move in environs as comfortable as those of A.M. West's novels. Their lives were not as gilded or glamorous. But at least their ends would not be as terrifying and violent. Because they would all end. It didn't matter if she was Aggie Miller, unpublished writer, living in her damp little bedsit and working in the coffee shop, or A.M. West, cool and savvy crime writer, or…

Or…

Who was she now?

Agatha Miller she was.

Agatha Miller. Editor-in-chief of Morning Star Publishers, multimillionaire, fêted by Hollywood, pursued by beautiful A-listers. A success. An unprecedented success, it might be said.

But who hadn't written a word of her own for - how long was it?

Thirteen years.

Thirteen frenetic years.

Thirteen…

She was brought back from her reverie by Layfield-Brookes:

"My dear, you wouldn't mind terribly getting something out of my briefcase, now would you? It's round the back of the chair."

His speech was slurred. It was a strain to get that much out, but Aggie knew that his legal mind was still sound. They were still working together. They joked that they were "partners in crime". She wouldn't let him suffer the indignity of seeing a younger man take his place in the company. He still signed off the legal documents. He was the only one she could trust. She laughed inwardly at this thought.

The manoeuvre involved brushing past the old man's good side. Aggie wondered how much this had been planned. Was Layfield up to his old tricks? She imagined his arm grabbing her, sitting her down on his lap. But even in his younger days he had never been strong, never physically robust. Always mentally as sharp as a hawk, though. He and Edith had made quite a pair. As did they themselves. She squeezed around the chair, and rummaged in the briefcase hanging off the back. In it, there was an A4 parcel wrapped in brown paper and tied with string.

"Edith wanted you to have it. Told me to give it to you later. I think it's later now. Said you'd understand."

Aggie started blankly, as Layfield's good hand reached over to take hers in his. It was shaky, a far cry from the covetous, confident gesture all those years ago.

"You have forgiven Edith, haven't you, my dear?"

She nodded, eyes cast down, mumbling a terse "Of course."

Rather like Lady Diana in her ill-fated affirmation of being in love on her engagement to Prince Charles.

She patted him on the hand and then made to open the parcel.

"Maybe you could look at it later, my dear. I'm tired. I need to get back home. Or rather, the home."

The waiters cleared the table of the detritus of the tea and Aggie paid the bill. Layfield-Brookes wasn't so insistent about these old-fashioned niceties anymore. They both had abundant supplies of money, money they had made together, so what did it matter who paid? They parted, not at the sweeping stone balustrade, but at the back of the hotel, at what would have been called the tradesman's entrance. The dark alleyway stank with the contents of the industrial-sized wheelie bins, overcooked cabbage from Sunday lunch, and the weekend drunks' toilet stops. The Grand had never updated its access arrangements. It didn't do inclusivity and would suffer for it. Its clientèle wouldn't struggle up the stairs or put up with being pushed through the hotel's dingy back corridors for much longer. The pair parted with a kiss on both cheeks and the taxi driver helped Layfield-Brookes up the ramp at the back of the cab. Aggie insisted on walking back to the office, as she had always done after their tête-à-têtes over afternoon tea at the Grand.

Although the parcel was burning at her breast, she walked unhurriedly back to her office on the derelict Georgian square. Crisp leaves played at her ankles on a rising breeze. It was dark already and the night was bright and biting. She might as well enjoy the clear weather while it lasted. It would turn soon enough. She allowed herself the luxury of lighting a fire, something that the spendthrift Edith would never have done. Her hearth was always empty. For Aggie, building a roaring fire was an act of rebellion. She would sit there all night with a packet of cheroots and a bottle of whiskey and weave her spiders' webs all over her apprentices' manuscripts. She wouldn't be going home tonight, there was too much work to be done, and it was set to be a wild night, the wind already getting up and the rain starting to slash against the rickety sash windows she'd never replaced. It was a Grade II listed building and each classically proportioned window cost a small fortune to replace. PVC was not an option. The myriad of media people that buzzed around her were always trying to persuade her to move to London, to have a more prominent address, but she enjoyed being hidden away here, incognito. They just didn't understand that it was part of Morning Star's mysterious appeal.

When the fire was blazing away nicely, Aggie settled down in her high-backed armchair, lit her first cheroot, and poured her first dram of the evening. She placed the parcel on her knee. As her fingers twitched at the strings, the knots only got tighter. She didn't want to move from her spot by the fire, the rest of the room was so cold by comparison. She took another sip of whiskey and heaved herself up and over to the big mahogany desk that so intimidated the little butterflies of aspiring writers who fluttered around her after being summoned by the heavy cream letter. Again, the marketing gurus were always on at her to move her HQ to some hermetically sealed glass capsule on the top floor of a status-driven phallus with views of the Thames, but Aggie knew better. Edith had taught her well. Edith's ghost was here in the mellow smell of wood polish, in the wallpaper yellowed by nicotine and in the boxes of damp papers where the once-crisp novels of aspiring young authors went to die.

She rummaged through the deep drawers, and found the scissors right at the bottom of the last drawer she searched. Edith would have ripped the parcel apart with her red talons of fingernails as hawks ripped out the entrails of their prey, just as she had ripped out the entrails of so many young authors' minds. It was, as she had sickly suspected, a manuscript.

Edith's manuscript.

"Of Love and Other Crimes, a novel by Edith Mulgrave".

She turned over the title page, and loose papers fell out onto the threadbare Persian rug. Letters from publishers. Rejection letters. A litany of scorn: "incomprehensible", "lacking in realism", "women's fiction".

She settled down to read with her whiskey and cheroot. She read all through the night, pausing only to brew coffee to alternate with the whiskey and cigarettes and to tend to the fire with log after

241

crackling log. It was getting murkily light as she finished the most astonishing and original novel she had ever read.

She sat still, took a deep breath and knew what she had to do. She put another couple of logs on the fire and stoked the flames. Then she tore page after yellowing page from the manuscript and one by one fed each and every painstakingly searched-for word, each and every carefully crafted sentence, paragraph and chapter to the flames. She felt sure that she heard a scream as each page caught light, the flames licking around the corners, the edges curling up in pain, and exploded as the martyrs had done at the stakes if they had been lucky enough to have a necklace of gunpowder.

Aggie searched deep in the back of the desk's bottom drawer for her own almost forgotten yet beloved novel. She clung to it as she walked out of the door of 37A Nicolson Street for the last time. It was light now and the morning was clear after the night's rain.

She woke Tony, her homeless friend, who had taken to sleeping in her doorway, with a mug of coffee and a

"You'd best be moving on. Here, get yourself a place to stay".

She placed Edith's burnished gold rings, which she extracted with difficulty over her gnarled knuckles, in his blackened hands and the paisley pashmina over his shoulders. Then she helped him up and watched as he shuffled away.

As she sat in her old-accustomed café, sipping her over-priced cappuccino, she watched as the fire engines sped past, went out with the waitresses to witness the funnel of black smoke at the other end of town.

There was much swiping at mobile phones and talk of a blaze in the abandoned part of town. Tweets about drug addicts squatting in the buildings there.

It had only been a matter of time before something like this happened.

What was the Council thinking?

Aggie smiled to herself as she slipped back in to her table, picked up her pen, opened her manuscript and began to read.

And write.

Thankfully, most of this was completed before the Necessary Measures came in, so it's merely meant a slight delay. Be that as it may - Woj, Poj, Moj, and a whole slew of gratitudinous emojis to all you guys. It's been Difficult Work in Trying Times. (I've gone with a capitalizing theme here so it's come out more *The House at Pooh Corner* than 'We shall fight them on the beaches', but sod it, I'm sticking with it, I find Pooh Bear more inspirational than Churchill anyway. Good job, given what we're stuck with.)

Cheers, everyone, and stay safe.

Meredith Blanchwater

Meredith Blanchwater was born in New Haven, Connecticut, but has spent most of her life in the UK, and has lived in Newcastle since she moved here to study in 2010. She writes mainly poetry, some of which has appeared in various publications, and short stories, of which these are the first to be published. She has also written an as yet unpublished novel and a short play in which she also played a part whilst at university.

Jane Carnaffan

Jane Carnaffan is an emerging writer from the North East of England. She enjoys working with a range of forms and has written poetry, plays and short stories. She also likes experimenting with diverse genres, including comedy, romance and sci-fi. While she writes fiction, she weaves elements of her own life and experience into her work and is drawn to social and political themes.

Aged 8, she was commended in the WH Smith Children's Literary Competition for her poem 'The Robin', which ended with the memorable line, 'Proud and large but small'. Her use of adjectives, she hopes, is a bit more advanced now. She recently won a place on an 'Introduction to Playwriting' course at the Live Theatre, Newcastle upon Tyne.

Her favourite displacement activities from writing are walking and drinking coffee.

She lives in Gosforth, Newcastle with her husband and young son.

Emily Chapman

Emily Chapman is an MA Creative Writing graduate, with both BA and MA qualifications from Newcastle University. Born and bred in Yorkshire, she is currently based within the West Yorkshire region, taking a break from education. Short stories, poetry, and creative non-fiction are her areas of interest, with writers such as Neil Gaiman, Deborah Levy, and Chuck Palahniuk being amongst her favourites. She draws inspiration from her semi-rural upbringing, science, and all things weird and wonderful.

Emily's poetry has previously been published in *Independent Leeds* magazine, but her pieces for InkyLab are her first published prose.

Aurora Cording

Aurora Cording is an ex-arts student currently living in Newcastle. She was born in Halifax, West Yorkshire, and a lot of the material in her work draws heavily on dialect, mainly

Geordie and Yorkshire, though she hopes to broaden her palette with travel and immersion in different communities.

As well as being an ardent LGBTQ+ activist and feminist, she also loves art, anthropology, and the natural world.

Peter Jones

Peter is a poet and writer of short stories who lives in North Wales. His poems have been published in anthologies by Cestrian Press, and by Scarlet Leaf in Canada, as well as a couple of community arts pamphlets based in North Wales. Peter's been published on-line at Poetry24 and been shortlisted for the Robert Graves Poetry Prize. He performs across North Wales, Liverpool and Chester.

Peter is a chapter contributor to the academic book *The Principal - power and persuasion in FE* (UCL). Three years ago his (English language) short story *Twm Golau* (Welsh for *Tom Lights*) won second prize at Wrexham's Carnival of Words.

Barry Marshall

Barry Marshall is a fiction writer based in Newcastle-Upon-Tyne. He is studying an MA in Creative Writing at Northumbria University and working on his debut novel and a short story collection. Barry can be found on Twitter under the handle @BJM_Writes.

Johnny O

Johnny O is currently unaccounted for and is very possibly dead. However, he hasn't let this interfere with his work.

Ann Ridley

Ann Ridley has written stories, plays, and poems since she was a child. From around the mid-Nineties these have been commended and shortlisted in various publications. Her plays and pieces for theatre have been performed at assorted venues around the North-East.

She worked as a primary school teacher, nurse, and actor to pay the bills. Her other interests include walking, travel (her experiences backpacking around India and Nepal resulted in a published account), Ann also participates in two dance groups for sprightly older folk, and is a member of a six piece Thirties band, playing the ukelele, melodeon and triangle for the sheer fun of it.

Sara Waymont

Sara is very much a Jack of all trades and, probably, a master of none. After completing her MA in Medieval Studies at UCL, she went on to become a Latin teacher. Since then she has served with the RAF, travelled to Afghanistan as a War Artist, trained as a Yoga teacher, worked with combat-injured veterans living with trauma, and written a book (*Yoga, PTSD and Me*) for everyone and anyone who is suffering from stress.

Sara's passions in life are helping others, learning, writing and teaching. She sometimes (when he's not travelling the world) lives with her former Royal Marine partner and their little black cat, imaginatively named Midnight. She doesn't live with her mischievous old pony Poem because, quite obviously, she's simply too big to fit in a one-bedroom flat.

K Weismann

Born in the light of a half-arsed torch and bat-shaped ever since, K Weismann is a loner and a loser and the best friend you never had.